ONE HUNDRED NIGHTS

AN ASPEN COVE SMALL TOWN ROMANCE

KELLY COLLINS

BOOK NOOK PRESS

CHAPTER ONE

Everybody lies; that's a universal truth. Beth Buchanan had been lying to herself for some time now. She was convinced she had the morning flu ... for the last fourteen days. But staring at the pregnancy tests lined up in a neat row on her bathroom counter, she could no longer fib to herself.

One test could have been faulty, but when all three gave her a positive reading, she knew she was good and knocked up. And Gray Stratton was the father.

"I'm going to kill my mother," she growled as she looked down at her super fans, which included a tailless dachshund named Ozzy Pawsborn, a mostly bald cat named Kitty Van Halen, and a toothless German shepherd named Gums and Roses.

"What the hell was she thinking?" She stared at her menagerie of pets—all rescues—all worth saving.

She railed internally at her mother and scooped Kitty into her arms and snuggled her frail body to her chest. Kitty's sweater caught on the button of Beth's polo shirt, nearly pulling it loose, but neither one of them minded because she needed comfort, and Kitty always needed warmth after losing most of her fur in a house fire. She wasn't much to look at with her scarred skin and patches of white fluff, but Beth thought she was beautiful because she saw the cat's fighting spirit in those golden eyes.

"I knew it." She swiped the tests from the counter into the trash can with her free hand and stomped toward the kitchen. "As soon as Mom said she poked holes in Merrick's condoms, I knew, but somewhere in the back of my mind, I hoped." Kitty wiggled in her arms until she put her down. "I know you don't care as long as you get your food." She wished her life was as simple as one of the pets who slept for twenty hours each day and only cracked an eye to eat.

She opened the cupboard and pulled out the kibble and cat food. It was a daily process to feed her critters. Ozzy was allergic to grain, so he got a protein and pea mixture. Kitty required extra nutrients to heal her wounds, so she added vitamin drops to her food. Gums had no teeth, so Beth soaked his kibble in warm water, making it easy to eat and digest.

They all sat in a row, looking up at her with expectant expressions. She put their bowls in three corners of the kitchen and walked into the living room.

Above her, she could hear her mother walking around the kitchen of the main house. Her sensible heels' tip-tap cadence was almost the same as Queen's "We Will Rock You" intro. The clap, clap, stomp of the beat rang through her head. Besides animals, she loved music, and that's how all this trouble began.

"Damn you, Merrick, why did you have to get shot?" That was it. When her brother got shot the last time, it drilled home how fragile life could be. While she was never a wallflower, she hadn't been much of a rebel either. That moniker would go to her feminist mother, who was probably in the front row when women started burning their bras. She probably held the torch that set them on fire. Elsa Buchanan was a force to reckon with, and Beth lived in her shadow all her life. Not that she was weak or mousy, but her mom's flame simply burned brighter—blindingly bright.

When Merrick was finally out of the woods, and she knew he'd be okay, Beth started living. She was never one to dip her toes in the water. She was a jump right in kind of woman, and that's how she ended up with Gray Stratton after a night of old-fashioneds and music. Who wouldn't love a man who could sing like an angel and play her body like an instrument?

She smiled as she thought about that night, but then her mom's heels moved on the floor above her head and brought her back to reality.

"No wonder Merrick moved three hours away." She tilted her head back and stared at the ceiling. "He had to get away from your constant meddling."

Beth considered her living arrangements. It was never ideal to live in the basement apartment, but it was cheap, and as a veterinary technician, she wasn't rolling in the dough. She made enough to put some cash away and take care of her pets, including a hamster named Trip and a betta fish named Mr. Spitz, for his graceful movement through the water despite missing half a fin.

She closed her eyes and pictured her mother drinking her second cup of coffee before work; the heat of her flame burned hotter and hotter until she knew if she didn't go upstairs and confront the issue at hand, she'd combust.

She slipped on her shoes and walked to the

door, calling over her shoulders to her pets, "If you hear screaming, don't worry, it's just me murdering my mother."

She climbed the steps and marched right inside the back door. With her hands on her hips and her head ready to explode from fury, Beth searched her mother out and found her in the living room talking on the phone.

"Oh my God," Elsa squealed. "While I should say I'm sorry, I'm not. I'm terribly selfish and so excited." She looked up and saw Beth standing in the doorway. "Come in, sweetheart. I'm on the phone with Deanna, and guess what?" Her mother rose from her seat and danced around the living room. "I'm going to be a grandmother."

Times two.

Beth tried to put on a smile and act excited, but her body shook more like she was having a seizure than celebrating the news.

She said, "Congratulations," before she mimicked an off-with-your-head motion to her neck. "Mother, I need to talk to you."

Elsa sighed, "Deanna, I have to go. Beth needs her mommy," she said with no lack of sarcasm, "but I'll talk to you soon." She giggled. "I can't wait to shop. What do you think of yellow and green for the nursery?"

"Mom." Beth's eyes hurt from the strain of the

dagger-like glares she sent her mother's way. "Now."
For extra effect, she thumped her foot against the
floor, but it was all for naught because the carpet ate
up the sound effect she was after. She looked
around the room, which was wall-to-wall bookshelves, just like in the library her mother ran like a
drill sergeant. She knew on closer inspection she'd
find each book labeled with the same Dewey Dec-
imal System her mother used as a librarian. If her
mother was nothing else, she was always in control.

Elsa said goodbye and hung up. "What is wrong
with you? Is it that time of the month? Because honestly, Beth, you've been off for weeks."

Her entire body vibrated with rage. She was
sure her head was about to spin like the girl
in *The Exorcist*. She'd already been vomiting whatever color of food she ate, so no need for the green
pea soup.

"No, Mom. I'm not on my period, and do you
know why?"

Her mother cocked her head to the side and
opened her mouth to speak, but Beth held up her
hand.

"Zip it." She'd never been that bold with her
mother. No one ever dared to challenge the great
Elsa Buchanan. "It's because I missed my period.
Do you know why that happened?" Her voice

pitched close to hysteria. "Because you got me pregnant."

The look on her mother's face was like someone smelling something foul. "How did *I* get you pregnant?"

Beth tapped her foot on the carpet and waited for it to click with her mother.

When Elsa's hand covered her wide-opened mouth, she knew her mother finally understood. There was a minute where her mother's expression tilted toward concern or maybe shock, but the mask of calm immediately went up, and her mother was back to her usual steadfast self. "I didn't get you pregnant. You're the one who slept with whoever the father is." Her mother's eyes narrowed. "Who is the father?"

"None of your business." Beth rushed forward. At five-foot-six-inches tall, she stood eye to eye with her mother. "I can't believe you did that." She raised her hands in the air. "What mother does that?"

"A mother who wants grandchildren." She smiled. "It looks like I'm getting a two for one deal." She tapped her chin. "If Deanna chooses green and yellow, what color do you want?"

"Geez, Mother. Are you listening to yourself? I'm pregnant and single."

Her mother waved her hand in the air. "I raised two children on my own. You could raise one."

Beth let out a scream that shook the windows. "You had a choice. I didn't." She fisted her hands and pressed them to her sides so she didn't reach out and choke her mother. "I bet you poked holes in the condoms to have us."

Elsa rocked her head back and forth. "Only for Merrick." She smiled smugly. "You were an immaculate conception."

"Which means you don't know who my father is. Is that why I don't know his name?"

"Because you didn't need him. You had me, and I was enough."

Beth raised her hands and gripped the roots of her hair. "But what if you weren't?"

"Stop being so dramatic. My point is that you're over thirty, and honestly, it's probably the right time for you to have a child. You can thank me later."

"Listen to yourself. Your habit of meddling in our lives just created two unplanned babies."

"I'll help you."

Beth shook her head. "Haven't you done enough? I don't need a damn nursery in green and yellow. I need you to stay out of my life."

Her mother stood tall and gave that be-quiet-in-the-library look. "That will be hard with you living in the apartment downstairs."

Beth placed her hand over her stomach. "I'll be out by next week."

"What do you mean?" The same look of fear that happened when Merrick got shot crossed her mother's face. She knew she was at risk of losing another child, but this time, the choice was Beth's and not some criminal with a handgun.

"I'm moving to Aspen Cove." She turned and walked to the door.

"What will you do there? There's nothing in that little town."

Beth whipped around to face her mother. "Not true, there's my brother and the father of my child."

"You think whoever he is will want to help you raise a baby? Let me tell you, one-night stands aren't interested in wives or children."

"You would know, wouldn't you?"

Her mother stumbled back as if pushed.

"Don't you think your brother has enough going on that he doesn't need another pregnant woman to care for?"

Mom was hitting below the belt and hurting Beth must have been a last-ditch effort.

"If you ever want to talk to me again, you'll stop interfering in my life, and that means you don't say a word to anyone about my baby. I get to decide when to tell and who to tell." She touched her stomach again. *My baby.* That was precisely what this situation would turn into—her and a baby. Men like Gray Stratton weren't relationship material. They worked hard and played hard. Dozens of women lined up each evening to experience a single night with the musicians from Indigo. Who didn't have "bag a rock star" on their bucket list?

She had to give it to him. He sure made a lasting impression.

"Not a single word, Mother." She turned and walked away. She'd always told herself she wanted to be strong and independent like her mom. Maybe she should have been clearer when she put that wish into the universe. She was exactly like her mother—single and soon to be raising a child on her own. She knew she needed to tell Gray. It was only fair to let him know he helped bring a life into this world. The question was, how would she break the news?

CHAPTER TWO

Gray Stratton pulled his guitar out of its case and waited for the rest of the band to show up. They weren't touring, but they still met several times a week to lay down tracks for the new album.

He strummed a song he'd been working on called "Life is a Lie." He was halfway through the first verse when Red walked in, grinning.

"Good night?" Gray asked.

Red went directly to his case and pulled out the instrument. "Dude, have you ever done twins?"

Gray shook his head. "Be careful, man, I'm telling you, women can't be trusted. They will lie and cheat and take you for every dime you've got." He strummed an out of tune chord to make his point. "Think of them as a bad note in a good song."

"Jaded much?"

Gray reached over to get his favorite pick—a pearlized, white one he got when the guitarist from Ozzy Osbourne's band tossed it to the crowd. He was only a teen, but he knew then he wanted to be a musician.

"I have every right to be. Allison is sporting new boobs that I paid for, and she's on the arm of that punk from Turd's World."

"It's Third World, and who cares? She wasn't the one for you. That's why you should take a tumble with the twins. Double the pleasure. Double the fun."

"Or double the trouble. Mark my words, some-day, someone is going to show up and say, 'hello Daddy,' and you're going to be good and stuck." He knew how that went. Only the one he married wasn't really pregnant. Allison lied to him just to get that ring on her finger. He knew she had duped him when she got to month six of her pregnancy and still had a flat tummy. Always all in for love, he tried to make it work. He'd fallen in love with Allison as he cared for her and their "unborn child." The problem was, each time he left for a tour, she loved everyone else, and he meant everyone from the pool boy to the gardener to the pizza delivery guy.

"It happened to me. It can happen to you," Gray warned.

"Nope. I always glove it before I love it." Red plucked out the start to "Another One Bites the Dust." When he finished, he held up one finger. "First rule is never take a woman's word that she's got it under control. That's code for, I'll call you in a few months with my list of demands. You of all people should know that."

He did. Allison played her part well to get what she wanted. She followed the tour like a hungry puppy tracks the teat of its mother. She was always waiting for him by the tour bus. He was never one to grab random girls; he enjoyed getting to know them. People's lives fascinated him. Everything seemed richer if there was a connection. Hell, most hit songs came from a single experience—usually heartbreak.

He considered the lyrics to "Life is a Lie."
You played me like a song.
The chords filled my heart with love.
Until you slipped and one note went wrong.
That's when your strings of deceit strangled my heart.

"Learn from my mistakes," Gray said.

"That's why it's one and done with me. If you don't know her, you can't get emotionally attached."

"You're such an asshole."

Red smiled as if he was proud to be one.

"I am what I am. I lay down the ground rules right from the start. You get one night, that's it. Make the most of it because it will never happen again."

Gray had recently taken on that attitude but in a limited fashion. A man could only stay celibate for so long, and he wasn't looking for anything long term. He had plans, and they didn't include a wife, children, or a house with a picket fence.

While he had the reputation of a player, he wasn't. If he walked out the door with a woman, it was to escort her to her car and send her on her way home. He'd then go back to his place and take in an episode or two of *Breaking Bad* because it was one of the few shows that had a main character with a life more pathetic than his.

"When was the last time you hooked up with someone? Maybe that's your problem; you need to get laid."

"Dude, do you have to be so crass?"

Red laughed. "It's part of my charm. Women love a bad boy."

"See how that worked out for you and Deanna?" By the look that shadowed Red's face, Gray knew he'd hit a nerve.

"Deanna and I were never a thing. What happened there is a good example of one and done mixed with poor judgment and cheap wine."

"You sure about that?" He wasn't sure if Red knew the difference between genuine attraction and simple lust. One emptied the gonads, the other emptied a man's soul.

"Yep, while I admit to being jealous because she moved on to Merrick so easily, it was just a gut reaction to losing a fan."

"You're such a jerk."

"And proud of it. What about you? I saw you slink out of the bar with that chick a few weeks ago, and by the way your hands were all over her backside, she wasn't getting a courtesy walk to her car."

He closed his eyes and thought about Liz. It wasn't the first time she'd crossed his mind. If he were honest with himself, he'd thought about her a lot. She was the first woman who snuck out of his bed in the middle of the night. She was true to her word; she wasn't looking for forever, just one amazing night as she passed through town. He did his best not to disappoint, but in the process, something happened. She'd put him in the position most musicians put groupies. She'd used him and walked away, and that made him feel dirty.

"You know, the one-and-done thing is not all

that great for the ego. I wonder if those women ever feel trashy."

Red looked at the clock. "Look, I'm not about to be some chick's conscience."

The door opened, and in walked Griffin, followed by Alex, Samantha, and Deanna. He watched Red's expression change as soon as Deanna entered the room. His friend wasn't immune to affairs of the heart. While he might not have been interested in a full-blown relationship with their manager, Deanna, it was apparent he didn't like her belonging to someone else.

"Hey guys," Samantha said. She waved a handful of sheet music in the air. "I've got something new I'd like to try."

Deanna opened her mouth to speak but closed it in a hurry and bolted from the room. She returned a few minutes later looking clammy and pale.

Red pointed to the door. "If you're sick, go home. I don't want you giving it to me."

Deanna let out a laugh. "Don't worry, you can't get what I've got unless you have a fertile uterus." She sucked in a big breath before blurting, "I'm pregnant."

Gray took in the look of shock on Red's face. "Already? Why would you do that?"

The entire band stared at Deanna as if that was the question of the day.

"I didn't do it on purpose." She shrugged. "Apparently Merrick's mom is gung-ho on becoming a grandmother soon, and she took it upon herself to sabotage our collection of birth control."

Samantha gasped. "No. Seriously?"

"No joke. She poked a hole in every wrapper to speed things along. God help the guy who took my future sister-in-law home about six weeks ago."

The blood drained from Gray's body, but no one noticed because all eyes were on Red.

"Why are you looking at me?" Red asked.

"Because you're the most likely candidate," Deanna said without a hint of sarcasm or hurt. It was just a fact. "And by the way Beth reacted to the news, I'd say there's a good chance you could be a daddy in about eight months or less."

Red shook his head while the blood rushed back to Gray's face. He was safe because Beth wasn't the name of the girl he took home six weeks ago.

"Nope, that wasn't me." Red glanced around the room at the others.

Alex threw his hands in the air. "Not me either. I've got a pregnant wife at home. Besides, Mercy is it for me. I haven't looked at another woman since she became mine."

"What a sap," Red said.

Deanna went over and hugged the drummer. "You're a good man, and Mercy is a lucky woman to have you, but the rest of you players need to know that if any of you messed with Merrick's sister and he finds out, he's going to kick your ass."

There was an audible groan from the band. Merrick was a mountain of a man. Just his size was intimidating but add in that he was a cop and carried a loaded weapon to work each day, and no one wanted to upset him.

Samantha laughed. "Be careful out there." She set her hand on her stomach. "It looks like pregnancy is contagious."

Deanna squealed. "You too?" She hopped up and down with excitement before covering her mouth and running from the room again.

"Shall we practice?" Talk of happy relationships and babies exhausted Gray. The only good thing that came from the conversation was confirmation that he didn't have to worry. Thinking about Liz, he realized she was nothing like Merrick in looks or behavior. She was sweet and kind and only five and a half feet tall, unlike Merrick, who was an easy six foot six. Add to it that her name wasn't Beth, and he was safe. There was one thing he knew with absolute certainty, he would not get hooked into another marriage just because someone told him he was the daddy. That last experience had taught him a valuable lesson—women will do almost anything to get a large divorce settlement and a year of alimony. He'd never be that idiot again.

CHAPTER THREE

Beth pulled in front of her brother's Aspen Cove home. It was a small house but nicely put together with its fine finishes and classic styling.

"We're here." She looked in her rearview mirror at the two dogs and the cat. The only one who seemed the least bit excited was Gums, who pressed his nose to the window. Kitty and Ozzy were curled up on the seat next to each other, looking green from the long car ride.

On the passenger seat was Trip, who nibbled at a carrot. Mr. Spitz swam in circles in the cup she'd placed him in for the ride.

"Here are the rules. We're guests in this house, so be on your best behavior." She cracked the windows a bit and climbed out of the car, leaving the animals behind momentarily, figuring she'd let Deanna know she was there first. Unloading her fur and fin family would be like emptying a clown car at a circus.

She walked up the sidewalk. All the way there, she considered telling her brother and Deanna about the unexpected pregnancy but kept it to herself a little longer. There were many reasons why she wasn't ready to share the news, mainly because she wasn't prepared for the questions or the judgment.

Merrick couldn't say much about her being a single unwed mother since he almost put Deanna in the same situation. They weren't married, but they weren't single either. The one thing she knew about her brother was that he would always take care of Deanna and their child. Beth did not know how Gray would respond. Nope, she'd keep this secret tightly contained until she was ready to deal with it.

At the door, she raised her hand to knock, but before her knuckles hit the wood, it flung open, and Deanna rushed forward with a hug.

"You're here."

"Yep, I'm here."

"Hey, sis," Merrick came around the corner dressed in his khaki uniform, a holster, and a smile. Beth loved seeing him so happy. "Hate to leave you so soon, but duty calls." He gave Deanna a peck on the lips. "You know, there could be a cat caper happening somewhere." He moved to the space beside Beth.

"More likely a cat in a cape," Deanna replied.

"So true, but if Mrs. Brown didn't have Tom, she'd be in town trying to dress someone else up. Her poor husband died just to escape the matching sweaters I heard." Merrick kissed her on the cheek. "See you later, and welcome to Aspen Cove."

She turned to watch her brother walk away and glanced at her Subaru to see her critters had crowded the window to watch. "They're here too and capeless."

When she spun to face Deanna, she saw the look of surprise on her face. "How many pets do you have?"

"Two dogs, a cat, a hamster, and a betta fish." When she called and asked if she could come to stay with them for a while, she wondered if her pets could go too. No one asked how many she had. Merrick should have known it would be more than one. Beth had been a rescuer all her life. It started with the baby squirrel she nursed to health after its mother abandoned it. She had at least a dozen birds she hand-fed over the years. There was the blind guinea pig she named Mr. Magoo. She once pulled a litter of feral kittens out of a storm drain during a deluge.

"Wow, that's like a zoo."

She shook her head and smiled. "Oh no, I left the monkey with my mother. He's the only one who can tolerate her."

"You're kidding, right?"

"About the monkey? Yes. About my mother? No." She glanced down at Deanna's stomach. Why she thought anything would be different, she couldn't say. At eight or nine weeks pregnant, there was no sign of the little peanut growing inside her.

Deanna looked past her to the car. "Do we need to get them?"

"Probably." She held her hands in the air. "While it's cool outside, cars are always hotter inside, and it's not safe to leave children or pets alone."

At the mention of children, Deanna placed her hand on her stomach. "Can you believe it?"

With a roll of her eyes, Beth said, "No. It's preposterous that my mother would screw around with someone's life. What was she thinking?"

Deanna stepped out of the house and moved toward the car. "I suppose she was only thinking about herself."

Trailing behind her by a few steps, Beth growled. "It's pretty damn irresponsible to change the trajectory of several people's lives simply because she wanted to be a grandmother." They reached the car, and Beth wrenched the door open. Gums jumped out first, followed by Ozzy. Kitty sat on the seat, waiting for Beth to pick her up. Poor thing had joint issues along with the severe scarring from the flames.

"What happened to her?" Deanna looked at the cat, then looked away.

She wasn't pretty, but it was her resilience that made the feline beautiful.

"House fire. No one thought she'd make it, but I saw the look of determination in her eyes when they brought her in."

Deanna's lips fell into a frown. "What about the owners?"

"They took one look at her and abandoned her. So many people don't want anything that's not picture-perfect."

"That's awful." Deanna opened the front passenger's door and picked up the hamster cage. "Where's the fish?"

"Front cup holder, not the coffee cup, but the Big Gulp with the holes on top."

"Ah, makes sense." Once she had the fish and hamster in hand, she shut the door. "I'm not sure how Sherman is going to take the invasion. He's never really been around other animals. In fact, I'm fairly certain he thinks he's human."

"They all do. Honestly, we're their people, and

when they look at us, they see themselves. Why wouldn't they think they're human?"

"Well, welcome to Aspen Cove." She led Beth toward the house.

At the door, Beth whistled for the dogs, who bolted toward her.

"Wow, how did you train them to come to a whistle?"

"Patience and understanding."

Deanna laughed. "Do you think that would work with Merrick? I've been trying to get him to take his shoes off at the door since he refinished his floors."

"I'd say you probably have to put a shock collar on that man. He's hardheaded."

After a sigh, Deanna said, "Yep, but I love him."

"Lucky you."

"What about you?" Her eyes went to Beth's tummy before they moved back to her face. "You okay?"

"Why?" she asked. "Did my mom call?" Fear raced through her veins. Had her mom broken her promise? She shook her head. It wasn't a promise but a dictate from Beth. It's the only thing she demanded, and she'd never speak to her mom again if she told Deanna she was pregnant.

"What? No. I just want to make sure you're okay" They walked into the house and shut the door behind them. "If you're moving here, it would be logical to think the argument you had with your mom was serious, and I was just checking on you. I have a mother too, and she can be difficult."

Beth let out a growl that caused Gums to bark and Ozzy to take cover. The little dachshund jumped onto the corner dog bed where Sherman sat like a king, looking at his kingdom. The poodle bared his teeth, which sent Ozzy scrambling to safety behind Beth's legs.

"There will be some adjustments coming, I see," Deanna walked over to Sherman and picked him up. "It's okay. You're going to have to get used to sharing. In about seven months, your life is going to change forever." She kissed the poodle on the head and put him back down. Sherman held his head high and disappeared down the hallway like he couldn't be bothered with the riffraff she brought in.

And that's precisely what Beth felt like. She was a beggar—some usurper who didn't belong but had nowhere else to go.

"Aren't you angry? You and my brother have had little time to be a couple, and now you're going to be a family because our mom is always meddling."

Deanna chewed her lip and let it pop loose. "Shocked ... yes. But once we got over the initial surprise, we're okay with it. Babies come when they want to, and this one decided it was his or her time."

"I'm glad you feel that way, but what if you didn't?"

They moved deeper into the house. Beth held on to Kitty in case Sherman wasn't a fan of cats. It was better to ease into these things.

Deanna walked into the kitchen and pulled two cups from the cupboard. "Herbal tea?"

"Yes, please."

"I've got mint and passion fruit."

"I'm staying away from anything dealing with passion. I'll take the mint."

Deanna eyed her like an inspector with a monocle. Had she already given herself away?

"You had a pretty powerful reaction to your mother's confession." Deanna poured loose leaf tea into a strainer and turned on a spigot in the sink with instant hot water. "Are you okay?"

Beth was glad Deanna's back was to her. Otherwise, she might have seen her face grow pale. When her future sister-in-law turned around with two steaming cups, Beth pulled Kitty to her face and pretended to nuzzle her. When she was confident the color had returned to her cheeks, she sat on a nearby chair and lowered the sweater-clad cat to her lap.

"Yes, I'm fine." She wasn't lying. She was as fine as a sailor tossed out to sea without a life raft. She was in a sink or swim situation. Thankfully, she'd had years of swimming lessons as a child. She might swallow a bit of water, but she'd survive. "I was reacting to the news as if I were you." She was her ... kind of ... she was pregnant and a victim of her mother's idiocy.

"Oh." Deanna cocked her head like an English speaker trying to understand a room full of foreigners. "I just thought,"—she waved her hand into the air—"never mind." She pulled the strainer from her cup and set it on a nearby saucer. "How long do you plan to stay?"

That was the question of the day. "I thought I'd try to make a go of living here." She smiled. "Half of my family lives here." She grimaced. "The half that I love and adore."

Deanna lifted her cup to her lips. Before she could take a sip, she set it down and sneezed twice in rapid succession.

"Oh, my." She eyed the cat and then scooted her chair back. "I was hoping I'd grown out of that."

"Allergies?" Beth asked. The way Deanna's eyes turned red and watered was a dead giveaway.

She nodded. "We had to get rid of our cat when I was a kid because I was so allergic that I'd break out in hives." She shook her head. "I'm sure it's just an initial reaction."

Beth's response was to pull Kitty closer to her chest. "Why don't I put her in my room?"

Deanna sneezed again and nodded. "That's probably a good idea. You know where it is."

Without haste, Beth rose and rushed her cat to the second bedroom on the right. When she returned, she found Deanna dabbing at her eyes.

"I'll look for someplace else right away."

"Oh, no," Deanna said. "I'm sure it will all work out." She let out a sigh. "If I hadn't already promised to sell Griffin my old house, I'd let you stay there."

"I'll keep my eye out for someplace new."

"You're welcome to stay here. Honestly, there aren't any rentals, and most of the houses for sale are nearly uninhabitable." She tilted her head back as if trying to get a sneeze to stay down, but she couldn't hold it back and let out a sound loud enough to wake Gums. He jumped to his feet with a bark, which started a loud cacophony of noise—a trio of dogs barking at different pitches.

Trip, who Deanna sat on the kitchen counter when she walked in, fell off his wheel from the stress of it all. The only one who didn't seem bothered by the noise was Mr. Spitz, who continued to swim around his cup as if nothing in the world could rattle his fins.

Beth drank her tea and thought about her predicament. She knew staying with her brother was a short-term solution to a long-term problem.

"I appreciate your hospitality, but honestly, I never intended to stay here for long."

"At the house or in Aspen Cove?" Deanna sipped her tea and stared at her.

"Not sure of either. All I know is I needed to get out of the basement apartment of my mother's house. It was time to move on."

Deanna stood and took their empty cups to the sink. "Do you need help unloading your car?"

With a shake of her head, Beth said, "Nah, I didn't bring much, just my clothes and what the animals needed. I'll get started if you don't mind."

"Not at all. I've got a meeting with the band. Your brother said to meet him at Maisey's around five, and he'll buy dinner."

At the mention of dinner, Beth's stomach flipped. Before she could embarrass herself, she rushed to her bedroom and went to the bathroom next to it. She turned on the faucet to drown out the sounds of her heaving. It turns out, her fourteen-day morning flu had now turned into the afternoon flu. What the hell was she going to do?

CHAPTER FOUR

Gray decided that morning it was time to move on. He'd agreed early on to move temporarily to Aspen Cove because Samantha's recording studio was there. So much for the winter plan. Now with Samantha and Deanna pregnant, he knew touring was over—at least until they popped, and the kids were old enough to deal with the separation. How long that was, he didn't know. What became apparent was he wouldn't be able to sit still long enough to find out.

He was like an oak tree. The longer he stayed in one place, the stronger his roots formed. Ever since Allison, he remained on the move, always traveling and touring to keep his mind busy. The months he'd been in Aspen Cove were already a challenge because it gave him idle time to think and ponder his past choices.

Every happy family in this town, and there were many, reminded him of what he thought he had. Thought was the most important word because he never really had what he believed.

He trudged toward the diner with a heavy heart. "Better to stay in motion."

"What was that?" Deanna asked, coming up behind him.

"Wondering what's all the commotion," he said, trying to stave off his thoughts. "What's this meeting about, anyway?"

He pulled the diner door open and stepped aside so she could enter first. "Samantha and I put together the new schedule." Her hand laid flat on her stomach. "With all the changes happening, we thought we'd gather everyone in one place. That way, we can answer questions and field concerns."

Yep, he knew this was coming. It was why he put out some feelers for a new gig. He'd still be happy to record with Indigo. Modern technology allowed him to record just about anywhere. It would never be as good as a live session, but only Samantha could decide if he was worth the hassle of piecing it all together.

Deanna led, and he followed. Pushed together

in the center of the diner were several tables. Red sat with his fork and knife in hand. The man was a troglodyte. Why so many women wanted him was a mystery. Maybe he was right when he said that women liked the bad boys. It seemed he was right. The worse Red treated them, the more they wanted him. He'd never understand women.

He took the seat next to Alex, who sat with his eyes closed and a smile on his face.

"What's got you all happy this morning?"

Alex opened his eyes and turned to face Gray. "What's not to be happy about? I've got a pregnant wife who cooks like Julia Child and a daughter who is determined to rule the world. I swear she's going to be CEO of something someday."

Gray patted him on the back. "Good for you, man."

The bell on the door rang, and he turned to see Griffin enter with a woman on each arm. He kissed each on the cheek and walked toward them while the women moved to a corner booth.

"The twins?" Gray lifted a brow. "Dude, don't be another Red."

Red chuckled. "Those aren't *the* twins, but I wouldn't mind a night with them."

Griffin shook his head. "No man, that's my mother and my sister."

Gray and Red turned to stare at the two

women. "Holy hell, your mom is hot. I swear they look like sisters."

"Don't even think about it," Griffin warned.

The ding, ding, ding grabbed their attention. When they swung around, Samantha stood at the end of the table tapping the water glass with a knife. "Put it back in your pants boys, it's time to work."

Griffin raised his hand like a kid in the classroom. "That's a disgusting thought. Those are relatives of mine. One is my older sister and the other my mother. Gross. Just Gross."

Samantha grimaced. "Sorry. Now back to why we're here."

All eyes fell on her.

"As you know, I'm expecting, and that means we won't be able to tour next year or probably the year after." She inhaled deeply and let it out slowly. "Having said that, I still plan on doing concerts but paring down the schedule."

A chorus of groans hummed around him. All he could do was silently tell himself he knew it was coming.

Samantha pulled out a chair and sat next to Deanna, who was taking notes. She was always great about sending them the minutes for the meetings.

"I know I pretty much blackmailed you all to come to Aspen Cove with the promise that it would be a short-time yearly obligation to record at the studio. I'm hoping the housing stipend I gave you will go a long way in helping soothe the sting that comes with a change in plans. I also know that some of you might want to seek other opportunities. I hope that's not the case."

Maisey sashayed over with her coffeepot swinging back and forth.

"Coffee y'all?"

All the guys turned their cups over, but Samantha and Deanna asked for decaf tea. Gray couldn't imagine all the sacrifices it took to become a parent. In hindsight, maybe he was lucky it was all a farce with Allison.

Samantha looked at Maisey. "I think we'd all like to order dinner as well. What's the blue-plate special?"

Maisey tapped her pen to her chin. "Ben is changing it up today and serving spaghetti and meatballs with garlic toast." She glanced around the table.

"I'm in," Gray said, followed by a chorus of "me too."

"You guys are easy," Maisey said.

"Yeah," Red said, "but we're not cheap."

Griffin laughed. "Don't let him fool you. He's cheap and easy."

The bell above the door chimed again, and a

shadow filled the space. On a second glance, it wasn't so much of a shadow as it was a brick wall called Merrick Buchanan. He walked inside, and the room felt smaller.

Gray turned to Deanna and watched her light up. He was glad she ended up with him because she was obviously in love.

Deanna bolted from her chair and threw her arms around Merrick's neck. Red grumbled something about getting a room.

Gray looked away, but a woman peeked out from behind Merrick. Not just any woman but Liz, the hottie he hooked up with about two months ago. He'd recognize her anywhere with that whiskey-colored hair and those sage-green eyes.

When Deanna stood back, she yanked the girl to her side. "Hey everyone, this is Beth, Merrick's sister."

Thankfully, no eyes were on him, or they'd see him turn gray.

"Does anyone care if they join us?"

No one said a word. Gray couldn't. He found himself speechless, thinking about Deanna's tale of compromised birth control. He glanced up and found Beth staring at him. Was she trying to tell him something with those soulful eyes? They spoke a thousand words on their night together, but it was more in terms of yes and oh.

He looked away. If Liz or Beth, or whoever she was, were pregnant, she'd let him know. Until then, he wouldn't borrow trouble.

Chairs slid to make room for Merrick and his sister. The former was sitting next to Deanna, leaving his sister to sit next to Gray. He shoved his chair back and crossed his arms over his chest.

He narrowed his eyes. "Beth, was it?"

She nearly sank under the table. They were having a cordial exchange of information on the surface, but the underlying message from him was *you lied to me*.

She cleared her throat. "Umm, yes, my family calls me Beth, but many of my friends call me Liz. My name is Elizabeth, so I answer to all three."

He nodded. It made sense, but it didn't stop him from being angry at her. She could have been more specific. Then again, once they hit his house, there wasn't much conversation. They spoke all right, but it was with their bodies, not their mouths.

She turned away from him when Samantha asked for everyone's attention again.

"Okay, I know you're hungry, and Maisey will be back with our food soon, but we need to iron out the schedule. I'll make it quick. Karaoke on Wednesday nights at Bishop's if you're available. We'll still do our scheduled concerts in Dallas, New York, Miami, and Los Angeles next year, but

I'll charter a flight. No more luxury buses. Questions?"

Gray wasn't sure if the timing was right, but he needed to let them know where his thoughts were.

"I might pursue something else." The table went silent, and all eyes turned to him. "I'm not leaving the band, but the logistics might be different. I'm weighing my options." He looked around the diner. "Aspen Cove is fine, but it's not the entertainment mecca of the world."

He scanned the group, and his eyes landed lastly on Beth, whose lips pulled as tight as his guitar strings.

"Okay," Samantha frowned. "You're still going to record with us, but you're taking on other projects?"

He nodded. "Yes. The band will always be my priority, but you know me, I can't sit still for too long. It drives me bat-shit crazy. Our touring lifestyle is in my blood."

Maisey walked over with dishes of pasta lining her arms. How she carried six plates in one trip was a mystery.

"Oh, hey, you two." She looked between Merrick and his sister. "I can put a rush on whatever you want to eat." She moved around the table, setting plates in front of the band members.

Merrick pointed to Deanna's plate. "I'll have what she's having." He leaned into Deanna. "Are you sure your stomach can handle all that garlic? Should I get more Tums?"

She giggled. "Yes, and yes."

Maisey stood behind Beth. "Who do we have here?"

Beth raised her eyes to look at the woman who seemed to mother everyone in town. "I'm Merrick's sister Beth."

"I thought I recognized you. You came in a time or two with your mom."

Under his breath, so no one could hear, Gray said, "She must not be a friend."

When Beth's eyes snapped to his, he knew she heard him, but it didn't appear that anyone else had.

"Nice to see you again. Are you going to be a part of the herd and get the blue-plate special, or are you going to lone-wolf it?"

She lifted her shoulders, and the slight movement shifted the air enough for him to smell her shampoo. It was fruity, like mangoes or something tropical. He smelled it on her pillow for days after she left, and it disappointed him when it entirely disappeared.

"I'll have the pasta."

"I'll let Ben know. What about drinks?"

"Water is fine for me."

"You got it." Maisey left, and a soft hum of intermittent conversation and the clanking of forks on plates took over the table.

Thinking it would be rude for him not to engage her in conversation, he turned to her. "So, Beth," he said with an emphasis on her name. "How long are you staying in town?" He was hoping it was only a day or two because the quicker she left, the better it was for him. She was sitting at least a foot or so away from him, and even at that distance, his body remembered her. Everything sparked to life, so he scooted closer to the table to avoid embarrassment.

"I've got some things to work out. I'll be here for a bit."

He swore his heart skipped a beat. Was that fear or excitement? He couldn't be sure, so he assumed fear at this point.

"Oh, are you okay?" He figured this was the perfect time for her to let him know if she was in any kind of trouble. The kind that took nine months to work out.

Instead of blurting, "Hey, Daddy," she chewed her bottom lip and nodded.

"Yep, all good here."

The conversation came to an abrupt halt when

a plate of pasta appeared before Beth. Silence accompanied the rest of the meal, but it didn't stop him from talking to himself. Inside his head, he had a thousand questions. One being, could he possibly talk her into one more night before she left or he did?

CHAPTER FIVE

For the last two days, Beth pondered Gray's words. "Our touring lifestyle is in my blood." That meant he was leaving, at least temporarily.

She laid in bed and weighed her options. She could not tell him, but would that be fair? Trying to put herself in his shoes, she knew she'd want to know, but she wasn't Gray. Telling him might put a wrench in his plans to seek other options, and she didn't want him to stay simply because his child was growing in her belly. But she always came back to the same result—he had a right to know. By not telling him, she would do exactly what her mother did to both her and Deanna. She took his choices away.

She threw off the blankets, making Kitty un-happy with the sudden whoosh of cold air from being exposed. Her tiny choked out meow made Beth tuck her back under the covers. She listened for any sign of life in the house, but the only clue anyone was living there was the smell of freshly brewed coffee. Months ago, that would have made her mouth water, but these days, the smell sent her running for the bathroom. She turned on the faucet to disguise the noise and kneeled before the toilet to retch. How long would she dry heave before this part of the fun was over?

After five minutes of nothing but nausea, she rose from the floor and washed her face. Just as she reached for her toothbrush, her phone rang, Ozzy and Gums started a duet of barking.

"Dammit," she rushed to the nightstand, hoping the noise didn't wake Deanna. She seemed to suffer from the intermittent all-day flu, and Beth was sure it exhausted her. Making a baby was hard work.

"Hello," she said.

"Finally." Annoyance tinged her mother's voice.

Beth had been ignoring her calls but didn't have time to look before she answered this time.

"Hello," she sighed.

"When are you coming home?"

She was still so angry that she couldn't imagine going back to the apartment. She knew if she were there, she'd spend every waking hour seething. Each time she heard her mother move around upstairs would only make her angrier about her mother's interference. Or maybe it would only clarify that she was right on so many levels.

She'd made a mental list of all the reasons she was pissed at her mom, but each one had an addendum that stated why the problem was ultimately hers.

Holes in condoms—she should have been responsible for her birth control and not stolen her brother's stash.

Unexpected pregnancy—probably shouldn't have chosen on a whim to sleep with Gray. Then again, he was hot and a musician and—

"Are you there?"

"Yes, I'm here, but I'm not coming home."

Her mother huffed into the phone. "Don't be silly. You're pregnant and single."

"Mom, you don't have to remind me. I'm well aware of my condition and marital status, but like you told me, if you could raise two on your own, I can certainly take care of one."

"I know what I told you." There was a pause. "But honestly, it's difficult. If I'd had other ... never mind. All I'm saying is if you move back home, I will help you."

Mom was trying to be nice, but that didn't change the situation. In her attempt to manipulate the world around her, she changed lives, and there were consequences for her actions.

"I can't. You were right. I'm thirty-two, and I should be able to stand on my own two feet. Coming here was my first step."

"But—"

"I've got to go. I need to find a job."

"Did you quit your job here?"

That was a story all on its own.

"I got fired when I asked for a few weeks off. It turns out they don't like their employees calling in sick five mornings in a row and then trying to take a few weeks off. Something about schedules and responsibility." Those early days of morning sickness were brutal. She couldn't understand how anyone gained weight during pregnancy when she lost everything she ate each day.

"Oh, honey. I'm so sorry. You loved that job."

Loved was the keyword. "I did, but I'll find another job I love. I've got to go."

She hung up and flung herself back into bed. She would have stayed there all day if she hadn't heard Deanna sneezing and sneezing and sneezing.

Gums sat at the door whining to go out and

Ozzy, being the follower he was, picked up the noise but an octave higher.

"Okay, I'm coming." She rolled back out of bed and stood right into her slippers.

She padded down the hallway where she found Deanna standing in front of the sink, making herself a cup of hot tea. When she turned around, Beth gasped at how bad the poor girl looked. There were hives all over her neck, and her eyes swelled almost shut.

"Oh, my goodness. I'll be out in the next day or so, and I'll keep Kitty in my room until then."

Deanna chuckled. "It feels worse than it looks."

"I'm so sorry." Beth let the dogs out the back door and rushed to Deanna, who stepped back.

"Don't take it personally, but that cat spends more time in your arms than it does anywhere else. I think I'll keep my distance."

The front door opened and in walked Merrick with a box from the bakery. Beth knew it was muffins because he brought them each day for Deanna.

"How are you feeling, love?"

Deanna smiled at him. Just watching how she melted at the sight of Merrick made Beth ache for more. She wanted someone to look forward to—someone who thought the sun rose and set on her ass.

"I'm doing okay. I called the doctor, and he said it was safe to take an antihistamine."

"Do we have any?"

Deanna nodded. "Yep."

Merrick turned to Beth. "Hey, sis. Look ... umm—"

Beth held up her hand. "You don't have to say a word. I'm getting dressed and heading out to find my own place."

"You sure you don't want to go back to Aurora? I mean ... there's more there in the way of jobs and dates and stuff to do."

"Mom's also there." She shook her head. "Nope, I want to be here so I can terrorize my big brother."

He leaned against the counter. "We have a vet clinic. Talk to Charlie and see if she can help you out with a job. Eden works there now, but she's got a little one."

"Holy hell," Beth said. "Is there something in the water here?"

"There's something here all right, but I'm fairly sure it has little to do with the water." He rubbed his chin. "If you can't find something here, check out Copper Creek. The commute would be a bitch, but at least they have more options."

She let the dogs inside and gathered up their food and bowls to feed them in her room. "I'll do my best to be out within a week. How's the rental market in town?"

Deanna laughed. "There's no rental market. All that's left are houses that have seen better days." She rummaged through a nearby drawer. "Here's the number for the developer who owns most of the properties in town. Please don't take his first offer and don't let him talk you into a place on Daisy Lane. They are all in pretty terrible shape. You'd be better off on Lily, Jasmine, or Pansy."

"Got it, stay away from Daisy." She looked down at the dogs. Sherman had joined the group but stood in the corner as if analyzing the situation. "Don't worry, Sherman, we're temporary."

As if the dog understood, he walked forward to say hello to Gums and Ozzy with a sniff of their backsides. It was the first interaction since he growled at Ozzy on day one.

"Grab a muffin before you head out." He wrapped his arm around Deanna's waist. "I'm going to take her to bed and make her feel better."

"Oh lord, I don't want to know." She grabbed a cranberry-orange muffin and corralled her pets toward her room.

"I meant I was going to get her to relax so I could put a cold compress on her eyes," Merrick said from behind her.

"Call it what you want. I know exactly what

you're up to." She hurried down the hallway and locked herself in her room. After she fed the beasts, she collapsed on her bed and cried. Her life was going up in flames. She didn't want to go back to her apartment, and she couldn't stay at Merrick and Deanna's. The only way to go was forward. Not that she couldn't take care of herself. She was completely capable of adulting, but no one had ever forced her to do it.

She dragged herself out of bed and showered. When she glanced at her reflection in the mirror, she resembled Deanna with her puffy eyes and red nose. She tossed on a decent outfit, told her pets to behave, and walked out of the house. She had a mental list to work through. First, she needed to find a job. Second, she needed to find a place to live.

She called Mason Van der Veen on her way to Main Street and left a message. As she walked past the corner store, she saw the woman inside taking a hammer to the wall, and it wasn't to hang a picture. Nope, she was releasing a good dose of rage on the drywall.

She moved past the store and the pharmacy to the vet clinic and walked inside.

"Welcome," a pretty blonde said from the counter. "I'm Eden, and you're Beth."

Beth walked toward the door. "How did you know?"

Eden giggled. "Your brother called."

"Ahh." She moved to the counter. "Then I guess you know why I'm here."

Eden smiled. "Yep." She set an application on the counter. "Fill this out. Right now, we're heading into winter but come spring, things get crazy with the house calls and the nearby ranches. I'm sure Charlie would love to have a hand."

She deflated, sinking against the counter. "Nothing until then?"

"Probably not. I only work a couple of days a week, and that's just to get some me-time. I've got a little one named Tommy. I love him to pieces, but it sure is nice to get away for a few hours a week."

"I bet." She hadn't thought that far ahead, but when the time came, she'd need a sitter so she could work. "Do you use a sitter?"

Eden shook her head. "No, Thomas, my husband stays home with the little guy. Why? Do you have a child?"

"No," she said. "*Not yet.* I was just wondering what the sitter situation was like around here. You must have heard that Deanna and Merrick are expecting."

"Yes, it's the talk of the town. Nothing stays hidden for long."

That was what she was afraid of. She needed to

get herself settled before her secrets became next week's gossip.

She took the application and folded it in half, placing it in her bag. "Thank you for your help."

"Anytime. I live on Pansy if you ever want to join me for coffee. I could always use the company."

"I'll stop by sometime." Beth truly meant it. If she were to live in Aspen Cove, she'd need to meet the people and build some friendships. She might be single, but that didn't mean she had to be alone. "Do you know anyone who's hiring in town?"

Eden tapped her pencil on her chin. "You might want to try Bishop's across the street."

Beth looked out the window. "The bait shop or the brewhouse?"

"Oh, the brewhouse. The bait shop will close for the winter, but the bar stays open all year round, and the owner's wife is due in a few weeks. He seems frazzled lately. He's got Goldie helping a few days a week, but with all the attention the band brings, the crowd is too much for Cannon to handle."

"Right." She turned toward the door.

She remembered Cannon from the night she met Gray. He was half of her problem. The man was busy and poured with a heavy hand, which meant she got tipsy quickly. "I'll go see him now."

She turned and waved goodbye before walking out the door.

At the curb, she glanced both ways and crossed the street. A peek in the window showed Cannon wiping down tables.

She walked inside, but he didn't look up. "We don't open until noon. I'm not feeding anyone's uncontrollable drinking problem." He moved from table to table, spraying cleaner and scrubbing tables.

"I'm not here to get a drink."

"The diner's across the street then. We don't serve food unless it's pizza by the slice on karaoke night."

Cannon dropped the spray bottle and let out a few choice words.

This was Beth's chance to prove her usefulness. She hurried to pick up the bottle and snatched the cleaning rag from his grip.

"Have a seat," she said.

She pulled out a chair and pointed to it before spraying down the table and wiping it. This was something she did all the time at the clinic—that and mop up pet accidents.

"What are you doing?" Even though he looked at her suspiciously, he did as he was told and sat. He collapsed, actually, right into the chair.

She took him in from the dark circles under his eyes to the fact he had on two different shoes.

"You look tired." She glanced at his shoes again. "I'd say you're pretty well spent."

He looked at where her eyes sat and let out another expletive. "Aren't you Merrick's sister?"

"I am, and I'm looking for a job."

His eyes snapped to hers. "You want to work here?"

There was no use lying to anyone. "Not really, but the vet clinic doesn't need me, so I thought I'd walk over here and see if you did. And by the looks of it, you do."

He rubbed his hand over his face. "Can't live on a few hours' sleep. Sage is uncomfortable because she's so huge."

"Don't let her hear you say that."

"I mean, she's ready to pop. My wife is like twelve months pregnant." He chuckled. "I wouldn't let her hear me say that either, but the truth is, she's due on Thanksgiving. If she's up, then I'm up. Poor thing is up all night. She's miserably uncomfortable with all the kicking and moving." He cocked his head to the side. "You want a job here?"

She shrugged. Here was as good as anywhere else. "As I said, you're not my first choice because I'm a trained vet tech, but I'm pretty sure I could pull a beer and pour a glass of wine."

"Do you know how to mix a drink?"

She smiled and pulled out her phone. "No, but

there's an app for that." She turned the screen to face him.

"Mixology?"

"Yep, give me a drink, and I'll tell you the perfect mixture."

He sat up. "Okay, tell me how to make a dirty martini."

She lifted a brow. "Seriously? I can tell you without the app. It's vodka, vermouth, the juice from the olive jar, and a couple of stuffed olives."

He nodded. "At least you didn't tell me to pour a glass of vodka and talk dirty to the rim of the glass."

"Someone did that?" She moved to the next table.

He kicked out his feet and relaxed against the back of the chair. "Goldie wasn't a bartender either when she started, and she didn't have an app for that."

"Big mistake. Give me a hard one."

He rubbed his whiskered jaw. "How about a brand old-fashioned sweet?"

She set down the towel and typed in the drink, then recited the ingredients. "In a rocks glass, you muddle the orange slice, maraschino cherry, cherry juice, and bitters. Add ice, then pour in the brandy, water, orange juice, and soda. Voila." She waved her hands through the air like she was chanting a magic spell.

"Fabulous. How's your sense of humor?"

She leaned against the table. "I've got a furless cat, a tailless dachshund, and a shepherd with no teeth. My hamster faints at any sign of stress, and I've got a fish with a missing fin. I'd say I've got to have a sense of humor to take on that mess."

"You'll fit right in, then." He pointed to the register where a cat sat lazily, swishing his tail back and forth. "That's one-eyed Mike. If you look over the counter, Otis should be there somewhere. He can't be bothered to get up and say hello, though, because he's tired too, and he's only got three legs."

Beth set the cloth and spray bottle down and took off toward the cat. She picked him up and cradled him in her arms. "Look at you." Her eyes went down to the dog curled in the corner. "And you, too. Oh my God, you both are beautiful."

"You like the damaged ones, I see."

She rose from behind the bar and nodded. "Everyone deserves love, including one-eyed cats and tripod dogs."

"And surly bar owners. At least that's what Sage says." He rocked to his feet. "Wednesday is karaoke night, and things can get a little crazy if the band shows up."

A feeling of giddiness washed over her, followed by a case of the nerves. She was doing this.

Her phone rang, so she set the cat back on the
register and looked at the screen. It was Mason Van
der Veen.

"Hello, can you hold for a second?" She didn't
wait for him to answer. Instead, she tucked the
phone to her chest. "I'll see you tomorrow. What
time?"

"Be here at five, and it will be baptism by fire."

"I can handle the heat." She hoped so, anyway.
She rushed out the door and took the call. "Sorry
about that. Thanks for calling back."

"You said you're looking for a place?"

"Yes, I desperately need a home to call my
own." She wanted to kick herself. Words like desperate wouldn't help her in the negotiation process.

"I've only got one house available. It's a fixer-
upper."

"Aren't they all in this town?"

"I'm nearby. Would you like to see it?"

"Yes. When can you meet me?" She glanced
across the street at the man who seemed so out of
place in his suit and tie. He held a phone to his ear,
and she watched him speak.

"I'm at the diner. When can you be here?"

She could see from his lips that he was Mason.
"Thirty seconds?"

He cocked his head in confusion as she walked across the street toward him. He looked around and stared at her.

"Hi," she said, holding out her hand. "I'm Beth."

"Mason." He pointed to his fancy SUV. "Hop on in, and I'll take you there."

She climbed into the passenger seat and took in the plush leather and wood trim; sure, it was the kind of car that did everything but painted a girl's toes. Mason Van der Veen didn't get a car like this from poor negotiations.

"Tell me what you're looking for in a home."

She considered his question. She had had little time to think about it. While she'd been squirreling money away for years, a benefit of living cheaply in the basement apartment of her mother's home, she didn't come to Aspen Cove to plunk down her life savings on a permanent home. Her hand instinctively went to her stomach. Her life was changing, and so were her needs.

"Right now, I need a place I can move into quickly." That was another tell that wouldn't serve her well. She might as well hand over her checkbook and tell him to write it for what he wanted.

"The house on Lily should work nicely for you. It's move-in ready."

"Perfect. How much is it?"

They pulled in front of a rundown home. Something about the neighborhood seemed familiar. She glanced around, and her stomach dropped. The house next door was Gray's.

"No, this won't work." She couldn't imagine living next to him. Then again, the proximity would give her a chance to get to know him. Wasn't it wise to see what kind of man he was before she committed herself and a child to a lifetime connection?

"It's the only house I've got. The only other one I can show you has a hole in the floor and a rodent problem."

She could do hamsters, but she drew the line at mice and rats. "Fine, let's look." What awful thing could come from a look?

They climbed out of his SUV and headed toward the door. All the while, Beth couldn't take her eyes off Gray's house.

"Yours can look as nice as that with a little elbow grease."

"And about a hundred grand in refurbishments," she said.

He shook his head. "All you need is a weekend of watching those home improvement shows, and you're set. Nothing is that hard to do yourself." He unlocked the door and stepped inside.

To her surprise, the house wasn't nearly as

awful as she expected. Maybe lowering her expectations was the key to happiness.

She moved around the small living room that led into a galley kitchen. The window over the sink looked out over a fenced-in backyard. It was a chain link but still enclosed, and that would help with the animals. Smack dab in the center of the yard was a massive oak tree she could imagine with a rope swing like the one she had in her yard back in Aurora.

"How much?" She moved from the kitchen across the worn wooden floors—floors that others had walked across over the years. She wondered if the last family to live here was happy.

"Aspen Cove isn't Aspen, so the property values are pretty low." He frowned. "I bought up all this property thinking a friend of mine was going to develop the lakefront with a mountain resort, but that fell through, so this is your lucky day."

He sounded like a used car salesperson. A stupid jingle from a car salesperson named Cal ran through her mind. *I'll stand upon my head 'til my ears are turning red.* "Just give me the price."

"I'll finance if you can write me a check for twenty percent down. I'm asking one forty."

She didn't have twenty-eight grand in her bank account. She had twenty-six, but she'd need furniture and supplies. "I'll give you one-twenty and not a penny more." She pulled her checkbook from her bag. "I can write you a check for twenty-four thousand right now."

"Deal," he said.

They went back to the diner to complete the paperwork. Three hours and several faxes later, she was the owner of a house on Lily Lane. She couldn't decide if it was a wise move or just another impulsive decision that would come back to bite her.

CHAPTER SIX

Gray watched the green Subaru pull into the driveway of the house next door. He saw the for-sale sign disappear yesterday and wondered who would buy such a shithole. He looked at it when he arrived in Aspen Cove. The bones were good, but that was about it. Everything from the plumbing to the heating needed to be replaced, and whoever bought it was wealthy or stupid.

He sat on the window ledge and watched as the driver's door opened. It was a woman who exited. Her head was down, and her hair fell over her face like a curtain, but the color of it was familiar. A deep chestnut brown that was richer than any chocolate he'd savored.

He couldn't take his eyes off the woman next

door. Like a bee to the queen in a hive, she drew him in. Curiosity was always his downfall. He liked information, and he'd stay right there with his nose pressed to the bay window until she revealed herself.

She stepped to the rear passenger door and opened it. Two balls of fur landed on their feet. One wagged its tail fervently, while the other, a wiener dog, wagged its butt since it had no tail. He'd heard of clipping tails and ears, but not once had he seen it done to a dachshund.

She leaned inside the car, giving him a perfect view of her back end. And he had to admit, it was a fine one. He loved a woman with curves. Bones were for dogs; real men enjoyed meat.

Watching her was like watching *The Price is Right* and wondering what was behind curtain number one.

She reached inside, and when she reemerged, his breath caught in his throat.

"Liz?" He couldn't believe his eyes. There she was, holding a bald cat and staring back at him. A weak smile lifted her lips, and her hand rose in greeting.

He pushed away from his window and walked outside.

"Liz?"

She dropped her head. "Just call me Beth. It will stop a lot of confusion."

He thought about her words the other day. *My family calls me Beth, but many of my friends call me Liz.*

He moved toward her. "Does that mean we're no longer friends, or are we family now?"

She looked up, and her cheeks turned pomegranate red. "We're neither. I mean ... I don't know you well enough to call you friend, and I know we're not related." Her nose scrunched while her lips pursed. "That would make what we did kind of creepy, wouldn't you say?"

"Yep, but what we did wasn't creepy at all. I'd be interested in a repeat."

She hugged the hairless critter to her chest and laughed. "Oh, no." She shook her head. "I lived on the other side for a night, and while it was nice, once was enough."

She hung her head again, and he couldn't see her expression.

He'd never had a woman turn him down, and something about her answer to his proposition stung.

"Girl, I'm like a Pringle. One is never enough."

She looked at him from the top of his head to the toes of his shoes. Her tongue flicked out to lick her lips like she wasn't satisfied with a single taste either.

"Too much of a good thing is sometimes just too much."

It was his turn to chuckle. "So, you're admitting it was good." His ego wasn't that fragile, but he needed to know she enjoyed him and their time together.

The cat squirmed in her arms, and the dogs circled her legs. "I wouldn't kick you out of bed for eating crackers." Her lips lifted into a sly smile. "I should get them inside."

Her smile dazzled him, and he completely forgot why he'd come out here.

"Did you buy the place?" He cocked his head to the side. "I thought you weren't staying."

Her head snapped back. "I told you I was staying for a bit."

"Buying a house says long-term not here today and gone tomorrow." He narrowed his eyes at her. "If I recall correctly, you said you were passing through town. Why didn't you tell me you were Merrick's sister?"

She huffed. "It wasn't important."

"Information is important. I would have liked to know you were the deputy sheriff's sister."

"Would it have changed anything?" She shifted

the cat to her other arm and reached inside the car for her bag.

"Maybe."

She moved toward the front door. "Maybe that's why I didn't tell you."

"I don't like people who aren't honest with me."

She seemed to pale before him. "We should talk." She looked past him to the furniture delivery truck pulling into her driveway. "But, right now isn't the best time."

"Okay, I guess I should say welcome to the neighborhood."

"Thanks, I'm excited to be here."

He shoved his hands in his pockets and took a step back. "You got the place inspected, right?"

"Inspected?" She let out a huff. "I'm not stupid."

He pulled his hands from his pockets and lifted them into the air. "Not saying you are, but that house has big issues with plumbing and electrical."

She frowned. "How do you know?"

Out of the corner of his eye, he saw the delivery guys walk forward with a clipboard.

"I almost bought that house, but it needed too much work."

She chewed her lower lip and let it pop free. "Yep, it needs a lot of work."

"Delivery for Elizabeth Buchanan?" The man looked down at his paperwork. "Looks to me like you've got an entire houseful coming?"

She nodded and slipped her key into the lock. "Come on in." she nearly tripped over the dogs. "Let me put them outside, and I'll show you where everything goes."

She nodded toward Gray before she disappeared into the house. By the look on her face, he knew she'd dropped the ball on the inspection. He hoped she was handy or wealthy. If not, she'd be in trouble, and Gray didn't borrow trouble.

CHAPTER SEVEN

A side view in the mirror didn't show a bulge in Beth's tummy, but her pants sure felt tighter. It could have been the dozen Little Debbie snacks she'd eaten in the last three days or the two take-and-bake pizzas she'd consumed in the same time.

"Today is the thinnest you'll look for the next six or so months." Gums and Ozzy always looked at her like she was speaking a foreign language, and she supposed to them she was. She wondered if different breeds had a different dialect or was the language spoken by dogs universal. What about cats?

She brushed on some blush and slicked on lip gloss before she walked out of her bedroom and into the living room.

The space was nice. It lacked the homey

touches like plants and pictures, but it had the essentials like furniture and a television.

She'd spent the week moving in and getting settled. She exhausted half of that time ignoring calls from her mother, who threatened to arrive posthaste if she didn't return today's call.

In the kitchen, she poured boiling water from the instant kettle into her cup and added an herbal tea bag. Kitty moved in a figure-eight pattern around Beth's legs.

"You hungry?" She glanced at the clock and saw she had just enough time to feed the beasts before she left for her shift at Bishop's Brewhouse.

"I'm nervous," she told her pets, who took their positions in the corners she'd assigned them.

She pulled out their food and prepared dinner.

"What if I make a terrible chocotini?" The thought made her giggle. Aspen Cove wasn't a froufrou martini location. The townsfolk were mostly salt-of-the-earth types who drank beer and cheap wine.

She put Kitty's food down first, followed by Ozzy's, and left Gums for last to give it time to soften. She made sure Trip had fresh water and food and sprinkled some flakes on the surface water of Mr. Spitz's bowl.

"You guys be good." She opened the door and got hit with a brisk wind. She reached for her jacket, which she'd hung on a hook by the door. So far, she'd lucked out, and the weather had been mild, but the clouds swirling overhead and the drop in temperature told her things were about to change.

She hadn't had time to call anyone to inspect the heater, so she hoped Gray was wrong about its condition. Even if he wasn't, there wasn't a budget for home repairs. She was down to three figures in her checking account.

With that grim thought, she walked out the door.

Gray was climbing out of his truck as she rounded her Subaru.

"How's it going?" he asked.

"All good." She pulled open her door and stopped to take him in. For a guy in his late thirties, he looked to be in his twenties. His dark hair was always perfectly in place ... except that night when she mussed it up with desperate hands. Each time she saw him, her body tingled as if it remembered his touch. "What about you?"

He lifted a couple of grocery bags from the front seat. "I went to Walmart, so I guess you could say I'm living the dream."

The only place she'd been to shop was the corner store, which seemed to have everything she needed.

"You get anything good?"

His smile weakened her knees. "Can't live on snack cakes and TV dinners forever."

Laughter bubbled up inside her. "Oh, I'm living proof you're wrong. Cosmic Brownies and Hungry Man dinners have sustained me thus far."

He walked around his truck as if he was trying to get a better look at her. He nodded and then smiled. "You wear them well."

A gust of wind whipped around her. The icy chill of it settled in her bones. "Is it supposed to snow?"

"Yep, I hear we might get six to ten inches tonight."

"Great." She tossed her purse on the passenger seat.

"Did you get that furnace looked at?"

"It seems fine." She shrugged. "It turned on a few times over the last few days." What she didn't tell him was that it spit dust through the ducts that smelled like a dead animal had caught fire the first time it ran, but at least it ran.

"Good to know." He hugged his bags to his chest. "I'll catch you later."

"I'm working at Bishop's Brewhouse for the time being." She didn't know what she'd do long term. She couldn't see herself pushing drinks with a big belly, but she didn't have many options right now.

"Save me a beer."

Her phone rang, and she waved goodbye before climbing inside her car and looking at the screen.

"Hello."

"Elizabeth, this is your mother."

"Yep, I saw your name pop up."

"Why are you ignoring me?"

She started the car and backed out of the driveway.

"Geez, Mom, I'm busy. I had to find a job and get a place of my own."

"You rented someplace." Her voice dipped as if disappointed.

Beth took a deep breath. "Deanna is allergic to cats, so I bought a house." She held the phone away from her ear.

"You what?" she screamed.

"Look, I'm thirty-two, and it's time to be completely independent. I mean, how is a child supposed to depend on me when I don't depend on myself."

It seemed like a lifetime of silence had passed, but it was only a block of driving. "I'm sorry I got you into that situation. Have you told anyone else yet?"

It was a tremendous step for her mom to accept

blame, but what she was asking was if she could break her vow of silence.

"No, I haven't said anything."

"You don't have to go through this pregnancy alone. What about the father?"

Beth took two calming breaths. "Wasn't it you who told me that one-night stands aren't interested in wives or children?"

"There are things you don't know."

She was a bubbling cauldron of agitation. "Yes, like who my dad is."

"I'm not doing this again," her mother said.

"Don't worry. I'm not doing it at all."

"Beth, don't hang up on me."

She pulled behind the brewhouse. "I need to go, Mom. I've got a shift to pull."

"Where are you working?"

"Bishop's Brewhouse."

"You're working at a bar?"

She killed the engine and sat back, resting her head on the seat. "A girl's got to make money."

"Come home, Beth. Don't make us both suffer."

"You of all people should know that there are consequences for our actions. You taught Merrick and me that from the time we were little. The consequence of you meddling in my life is distance, and the consequence of my being impulsive and irresponsible is pregnancy. We are both going to have to live with our choices."

"We need to talk, honey." Her mom only brought out the sweeties and honeys when she couldn't bulldoze her way to submission.

"Yes, but not right now because I'm starting my first shift in five minutes. Love you." She hung up before her mother could say more.

She pulled up the mixology app on her phone, tucked it into her pocket, got out of her car, and walked in the back door.

"Oh, my goodness," the woman squealed from behind the bar. "You must be Beth."

Before she knew it, the pretty little blonde wrapped Beth in her arms.

"Umm," she wiggled herself free and stepped back. "Yep, I'm Beth, and you are ..." She tried to remember the name of the woman Cannon had told her about the day she got the job.

"Goldie." She bounced like an out-of-control ball. "I'm Goldie."

Beth wondered if Goldie was naturally exuberant or if she'd taste-tested every bottle of booze in the place before her shift.

"Nice to meet you. Is Cannon around?"

"Nope, Sage might be in labor."

Beth's eyes grew wide. "Oh, wow. That's..." She wasn't sure how to finish that sentence. She'd been reading up on pregnancy ever since the day she got her triple diagnoses, and labor didn't sound like much fun, but neither did swollen ankles and backaches.

"Exciting, right?"

"Right." Beth looked around. "Are you going to train me?"

Goldie giggled. "It's kind of like the blind training the blind, but we'll give it a go."

For the next fifteen minutes, Goldie gave her the low-down on how things worked around there.

"I've got this great app." She pulled her phone from her pocket.

"I heard." She pointed to her head. "I have to keep everything up here."

The door opened, and three men walked inside.

"Locals?" Beth asked.

Goldie gave them a look and shook her head. "Nope, but they're cute. I find the cute ones tip a little better if you stroke their egos."

Beth laughed. "Well, I won't be stroking anything else."

Goldie laughed. "You're a funny one. I'm going to like you." She pressed a tray, a pen, and an order pad into Beth's hand. "Go get 'em, tiger."

"You want me to take their order? What if I mess up?"

Goldie cocked her head. "You can't do any

worse than me. I spilled a tray of drinks and caused a fight."

She held the tray to her chest and inched toward the group.

"Hey, guys. What will it be?"

"What's on tap?" The ginger next to her asked.

Feeling like a deer caught in the headlights, Beth glanced at Goldie, who pointed to the tray. When she looked down, she saw the names of beers written there.

Feeling more confident, she rattled off the list, starting with Firestone and ending with Blue Moon.

They all settled on Michelob, which made her wonder why they even asked. As the night progressed, she got more comfortable with the bar's offerings and fell in love with the tips. She'd never considered waiting tables before, but having a steady flow of cash was a plus.

By nine, the place was mostly empty.

"Is it normally like this?"

"No," Goldie said and pointed to the window. "The weather is crap, and people stay home."

When she glanced out the window, she saw the snow was falling like a white blanket. Thankfully, her heater worked, or she and the menagerie would be in for a frosty night.

The door opened, and in walked a snow-covered Cannon followed by her brother.

"Look what I found lurking outside," Cannon said. "It's a good thing I never had a sister."

"Hey," Merrick said. "Just finished my shift, and I'm making sure she's okay to get home."

Beth smiled. She loved the way her brother always looked out for her. It was part of the reason she came to Aspen Cove. Merrick was a solid influence in her life, and he'd be there when she needed him the most.

"I'm good. Go home to Deanna—you look wiped out."

"It was a long day. As long as you're sure you're okay."

"I'm fine."

Merrick smiled before he walked out the door.

"Do we have a baby yet?" Goldie asked.

Cannon stomped his boots on the front mat and shook his head, sending out a shower of white flakes and water droplets.

"False alarm."

"When is she due?" Beth asked.

"Thanksgiving Day." He held up his hand. "And don't even go there about the bun in the oven or basting the bird. I've heard it all."

Beth hadn't given the calendar much thought,

but the holidays were right around the corner with Thanksgiving in a few weeks.

"Why don't you two head on out. I'm going to close up early. Anyone coming in now probably shouldn't be here, anyway."

Goldie rushed toward the hallway that led to the parking lot. "You don't have to ask me twice." She raised her hand and waved goodbye. "That mountain road is a killer during these storms."

Cannon nodded. "Tell Tilden hello for me and tell him I need some wood when he's got a chance."

Beth's ears perked up. "Who's Tilden, and can I get wood too?"

Goldie walked back. Her smile was like a full moon lighting up her face. "Tilden is my mountain man, and he delivers wood for Zachariah, who finally gave up moonshining."

Beth lifted a brow. "We have moonshiners in these parts?"

Cannon shrugged. "We used to until Zachariah's still blew up the last time, and he nearly lost an arm, so now he's just selling firewood."

"I'll let Tilden know you both need firewood."

Beth hated to ask, but she had to. "Is it expensive?"

"About three hundred for a cord, but that will last you all winter most likely."

That three figures in her bank account would

quickly disappear if she continued to have unexpected expenses, but warmth was a necessity.

"Okay. Sounds good." She knew if things got dire, she could ask Merrick for a loan.

Goldie skipped out before anyone could say another word.

"I'll wipe the tables before I go." There wasn't a single customer in the joint, so it was easy to collect the empties and clean up at the same time.

"How'd it go for you?"

"It was great. Probably a good day to start since it was slow."

"Make any money?"

She couldn't buy an island and retire, but she was happy. "Yep, I'm walking away with about sixty dollars."

Cannon frowned. "Yeah, that was slow then."

Beth's heart rate sped. If making sixty dollars was a slow night, she couldn't wait to see what a busy night made her. She only made fifteen an hour working as a vet tech, and tonight she worked four hours and made the same. She couldn't complain.

"It was great."

"Come back tomorrow night, even if the weather doesn't clear, it should be busy because it's karaoke night."

"Brings out the crazies?"

Cannon laughed. "There's a pop star in all of

us." He washed the dirty glasses. "You really should head out. The roads are icing up."

She wiped off the tray and set it on the back counter and gave Mike a pet.

"Thank you for giving me this job. I appreciate it."

He followed her to the back door. "In truth, it was more for me than for you, but I'm glad it helps. See you tomorrow at five."

By the time she made it home, there was an easy six inches on the road, which ate up all the noise, causing an eerie silence to fall over the town.

As if he heard her arrive, Gray opened his door. She was about to say hello when he reached out and grabbed a few logs from his front porch, and slipped back in. He hadn't been paying any attention.

She glanced up at the white plumes of smoke billowing from the top of his chimney and breathed in the comforting smell of the wood fire. Oh, how she wished she had the cord of wood now.

Just the twenty steps to her front door chilled her to the bone. Her hand shook as she turned the key and opened the door. Usually, all three animals would wait for her, but they were nowhere in sight.

"Where are you guys?" She flipped the switch, and the overhead light flickered to life. Her breath hung in the air like a cloud, and her heart skipped a beat. "Gums? Ozzy? Kitty." Heading to the thermostat, she saw it was just over forty degrees, and panic set in. She cranked the dial to seventy, hoping the heater would kick on and warm things up fast, but nothing happened. She listened for the clang of the compressor.

She had to check the breaker, but first, she needed to find her babies. "Hey, guys." A thorough look at the living room and kitchen turned up nothing. She rushed down the hallway to her bedroom and breathed out a sigh of relief when she saw the covers on her bed move. Animals were smart. Hers had burrowed under her blankets and used each other for warmth.

"I'm so sorry." Tears sprang to her eyes while guilt at nearly freezing them to death ate at her.

She sat on the edge of the bed and peeled back the covers, revealing first Gums, who curled around Ozzy and Kitty. She felt the warmth of their coats and wished she could crawl next to them, but she needed to figure something out and fast, or they'd be in big trouble.

"Stay here. I'm going to check the breaker." All three heads popped from the covers and gave her a you're-crazy look before ducking back under.

She pulled her coat tight around her neck and stepped out the front door. She knew the breaker box was on the side of the house nearest Gray's. Once she was there, she yanked and tugged, but it wouldn't open. She pounded on it with her palm and let out a yelp when it stung.

"Dammit, open up."

With her phone in her hand, she fiddled until the flashlight came on.

"You need to push in the lever."

She jumped a foot in the air, and both hands went to her chest while her phone flew from her hands and disappeared in the snow. "Don't sneak up on me." She whipped around to find Gray standing behind her. He blew into the cupped palms of his hands. "Cold out tonight."

"You think?" She shuffled to where she thought her phone disappeared. After a few seconds of digging, she found it, but the flashlight wouldn't turn back on. "Can anything get worse?"

The chuckle next to her reminded her she wasn't alone.

"I've learned in my life not to ask that question; it's like you're begging for trouble."

Something between a groan and grunt left her mouth.

I'm standing next to trouble.

"Can you open this?"

"I can." A smile lifted the corners of his lips, but he didn't move.

"Will you open it?"

He stepped forward. "Oh, you want my help to open it. I thought you asked if I was capable."

"Don't be an ass. While you give me a hard time, I'm liable to freeze to death." *And so will your kid.*

"It's like this." He leaned over her, pressing his chest against her back, and every neuron fired a message that said, *hello.* "Press on this lever and then pull."

The metal box screeched as it opened. "Is there a breaker that's tripped?" At the word tripped, she took off running toward the house. While the dogs and cat had each other, all Trip had was a toilet paper roll and shaved wood.

"Where are you going?"

She didn't say a word, only pushed through the front door and straight to his cage. "Hey, buddy?" She tapped on the cage and peeked in the corners to see if he'd buried himself. When the shavings moved, she said, "You're okay." She panted through an open mouth like she was practicing for the birth of a child.

"You okay?"

Her hand slapped against her chest, and she spun around to face him. "I told you to stop sneaking up on me."

"I knocked, but you didn't answer."

"I was in a panic."

He pulled his coat tighter around his body, which was a shame really, because Gray had an impressive body, and she was sure her temp would increase a few degrees from the sight of it.

"It's freezing in here." He raised his hand in the air. "I bet it's colder in here than it is outside."

"The thermostat says it's in the forties."

"Told you the heater was shot."

"And I told you it worked the other day."

"No, you told me you weren't stupid, and you had it inspected." He moved to the closet, where the heater sat as useless and cold as an iceberg. "It's so cold in here, you could almost freeze water."

At the mention of water, her stomach dropped, and she spun around and ran to the kitchen, where she found Mr. Spitz belly up in his bowl.

A plaintive wail rose to choke her, and all that came out was a strangled cry. She pulled the bowl to her chest and slid down the wall. The movement caused the water to slosh over the side and drench the front of her jacket.

"What the hell is wrong with you?"

She looked up through teary eyes. "I murdered my fish."

CHAPTER EIGHT

"You're crying over a fish?" Gray couldn't believe what he was hearing.

She sucked in a shaky breath and looked down at the bowl. "Mr. Spitz died because the house got too cold. I basically made him a fishsicle."

He stood over her while she fell to pieces. Women's emotions weren't something he knew how to navigate. Sure, he had his boss Samantha and the band manager Deanna who occasionally got emotional. Other than them, he had little experience outside of Allison, who had been a master at manipulating them. Still, Beth's tears were real, and they tugged at his heart.

"I told you the furnace was shit."

She looked up at him with tears running down

her cheeks. "I know. I'm stupid, and I acted impulsively." She ran the sleeve of her jacket across her face, leaving a black streak on the light material. "Now I'm screwed."

Getting a kink in his neck from looking down, he moved next to her and slid down the wall to sit beside her.

"It will be okay." He took the fishbowl out of her hands and set it aside. There was no use crying over a dead fish.

"No," she shook her head. "Nothing is going to be okay." She scrubbed her hands over her face and let them flop to her lap. "Everything is a mess because I didn't think before I leaped."

He glanced around the house, looking for her other pets. "Don't you have dogs and some kind of enormous rat?"

She nodded. "I have two dogs, and you know it's not a rat. Kitty only looks like a rat because she's missing most of her fur. They are hiding under my covers. I also have a hamster with a fainting disorder who has buried himself in a mound of wood shavings."

"You're a stray collector."

"I've been called worse."

He chuckled. "So have I."

She leaned toward him and rested her head on his shoulder. "What am I going to do?"

He swung his arm over her shoulder and pulled her closer. He was cold, and since she was wet, she had to be freezing. At least that's what he told himself, but maybe the truth was he liked the way she felt beside him. "You take it one day at a time, and one problem at a time. You can't solve everything right this second, so let's start with the most pressing issue, which is the heat."

"Was the breaker sprung?"

"No, they were all fine."

"Then I'm done for. I have limited resources, and I spent them buying this hunk of junk."

She turned toward him, which almost moved her into his lap. "You probably already know this, but when you turn on the water, it comes out orange for the first thirty seconds."

He wanted to repeat that he told her so but knew it would serve no purpose except to bring on more tears.

"Do you have firewood?" He shifted away and stood, then offered her a hand up.

"No." Her chin fell to her chest. "I inquired about it a few hours ago. I guess someone named Zachariah offers it, and Tilden, Goldie's guy, delivers."

A shiver ran through him, which meant it was getting colder in the house by the moment. "This is your lucky day because I have firewood. If we get a good one started, it will warm the entire house and get you through to the morning when you can call someone out to look at the furnace. However, it needs a new one. I'm fairly certain a temporary repair can help until you can figure out a long-term solution." He didn't know if it was salvageable, but at this point, it didn't matter. She needed to get through this night. She could worry about all the others tomorrow.

A spark of hope lit her eyes. "You'd loan me some firewood?"

He cupped her face and wiped the remaining tears away with his thumbs. "I'll give you some firewood."

She threw herself at him and hugged him tightly. "Thank you."

His arms naturally surrounded her. They stood for a moment until he felt the water from her jacket seep through his.

He stepped back. "I'll get the firewood. You need to take that jacket off before you turn into an icicle."

He stepped around her and walked out the door. At his house, he grabbed an armload of wood. He figured once he got the fire started, he could bring more over to hold her through the night.

At her door, he knocked with the toe of his boot, and she opened it immediately.

"You're a lifesaver."

"I came a little late for the fish." He glanced at the bowl still sitting on the floor and reminded himself to flush the carcass before he left. He was sure if he didn't, she would cry over it all night. "Do you know how to start a fire?"

She looked at him and then to the fireplace. When her eyes returned, her expression was as vacant as a mannequin.

"I'll take that as a no." He moved to the fireplace. "Do you have a newspaper?" When her shoulders fell, he chuckled. "I'll be right back."

He ran across her driveway to his house to get some kindling. When he returned, she was on her knees in front of the fireplace.

"The key to a fire is airflow and getting a good start with kindling, whether that's newspaper or small sticks." He kneeled beside her and pointed to a handle at the top of the fireplace. "This is the flue and needs to be open so the smoke can rise and exit the chimney."

He opened the flue with a firm tug, and a cloud of debris that contained everything from leaves to twigs to bird feathers came down.

They both jumped back and waited for the dust to settle. "You're going to need a chimney sweep."

She groaned. "Of course, I will."

He cleaned up the mess and set about creating a

teepee of sticks, all the while explaining what he was doing and why.

"Were you a Boy Scout?"

He puffed out his chest. "Yes, but I bailed after I got my Arrow of Light award. It was way too much work." He pulled a lighter from his pocket. "Are you ready?" Out of the corner of his eye, he glimpsed a giant furball. "Who's that?"

She smiled. "That's my shepherd Gums and Roses."

Surely, he misheard her. "Did you say Gums and Roses?"

She silently nodded. "Yes, apparently I have a thing for rock stars." A blush flushed across her cheeks.

He loved her sense of humor. Naming her dog Gums and Roses proved she had a good one. He glanced at the dog and saw that it wasn't alone. The tailless wiener dog had joined him. "Who's that guy?"

Beth got up and walked to her fur family. "This guy is Ozzy Pawsborn." She bent over and scooped up something from behind the dogs. When she turned, she held a sweater covered cat. "And this is Kitty Van Halen."

What started as a chuckle turned into a laugh that shook his shoulders. "Let me get this straight. You've got Gums and Roses, Ozzy Pawsborn, and

Kitty Van Halen." He looked at the fish. "What's his name?"

She smiled. "Oh, he was Mr. Spitz, like Mark, the Olympic swimmer." She pointed toward the kitchen. "And the hamster is named Trip."

It took him a moment to remember what she said about it having a fainting disorder. "I get it ... trip. Very funny."

"We can't all be rock stars."

"Thankfully, no," he said. "We're an awful bunch."

She stared at him for a minute. "You know that night we spent together?"

"Yes. I do. I never forget a face or a ..." He took her in from the top of her head to the tip of her toes. She had changed into a form-fitting sweater that outlined her features well. Beth was a beautiful woman, and he'd considered another night with her, but now that she lived next door, he realized what a bad idea that would be. "Let's put that behind us." He lit his lighter and held it to the kindling.

"I need to—"

"Holy hell," he said, cutting her off. He watched the smoke rise and then come back into the room as if there was a fan blowing it backward. "We've got a problem."

"What's the problem?" She fanned the acrid smoke away from her face.

The fire grew larger, and the room filled until they were both choking. If he didn't put the fire out, the entire house could go up in flames. He grabbed the closest thing to them: the fishbowl, and he dumped it on the building flame. There was a hiss, and a sizzle, followed by a scream.

"How could you?" She moved toward the fireplace, but he pulled her back.

"I had to. It was that or let your house burn down. There's something seriously wrong with your chimney. What fell through is probably only the start of what can only be a major backup."

"You fried my fish. All you need are chips and you'd have a meal." She rushed around and opened the windows to let the smoke out, but that only let the cold air in, and she hugged the cat closer to her body.

"Geez, Beth, I'm sorry. I was just trying to help."

Her shoulders slumped. "I know. I know. I apologize, but it's been a stressful day, and it's only getting worse. No heat, no fire, no fish."

He walked into the kitchen and picked up the hamster cage. "Let's go." He started for the front door.

"What?" she asked. "Go where?"

He knew he'd regret this, but what else could he do? "My house. It's not like you haven't slept there before." He looked into the cage. "What do you say, Trip? Care to get warm." He glanced toward the door where the two dogs stood, eyeing the humans like they'd lost their minds. "Come on." He patted his thigh, and the dogs ran toward him.

"They never come to anyone."

"Well, for all it's worth, kids and dogs like me. Now let's go before we freeze to death."

CHAPTER NINE

How in the hell did her life get so damn complicated? Beth watched her animals follow Gray out the door. If Kitty weren't trapped in her arms, she would have been right there with them. He had that kind of magnetism that attracted everyone around him.

"Don't mind me, I'll just scrape my fish from the hearth and grab what I need for the night." She looked around the house. The smoke was gone, but her breath hung like a cloud in the air. Each minute she stood there, she got colder until she was sure her bones had turned to ice.

She tucked Kitty inside her sweater. After a bit of wiggling, her little head popped out of the neck.

"Let's take care of Mr. Spitz." She glanced at

the pile of muddy ash, looking for him, and found him sitting in a puddle of mud in the corner. It just broke her heart. She was responsible for his death, but Gray got credit for the grilling or poaching. At this point, she wasn't sure.

Kitty grunted when Beth bent over to scoop the fish into her palm. Usually, she would have found him a nice box and buried him in the yard, but the ground was most likely frozen under the inches of snow.

She walked to the bathroom and justified the flushing by telling herself he was a fish and belonged in water, but as she watched him swirl around the bowl and disappear, she couldn't swallow the lump lodged in her throat.

"Beth?" Gray called from the living room. "Are you coming?"

She swiped at her eyes. They felt heavy and full, but she shed no tears. It was probably too cold for her body to release them.

"I'm in the bathroom gathering my things." She grabbed her toothbrush before moving into her room for a change of clothes and her Hello Kitty pajamas. "Can you help me with the litter box?"

The thud of his boots echoed down the hallway until he appeared at her doorway. "Is that all you need?"

She shoved what she collected into a bag and

pulled it over her shoulder. "It's just for a night." She moved toward him. "You don't have to do this, but I'm grateful for the save."

He chuckled. "This I can do." He eyed the cat box in the corner and moved toward it. "Anything beyond this, and I fear I'd disappoint you."

There he was again, making sure she didn't get the wrong idea about who he was and what they were together. He wasn't the only one who could distance themselves.

"Well, as I said before, you were a bucket list item. I've checked that off." When his jaw dropped, she walked past him and down the hallway. "Are you coming?"

He followed her out the door and shut it behind him. She slowed her pace to allow him to take the lead. They were going to his house, and therefore he should enter first.

At the door, he stepped aside so she could go before him. What she saw surprised her. The dogs were lying in front of the hearth on a blanket. A bowl of water sat nearby.

He moved past her, shut his door, and set the litter box in the corner. "Will they get into this?"

She shook her head. "No." Her animals weren't normal. They didn't scavenge litter boxes for snacks; they waited for the good stuff.

Kitty squirmed inside her sweater, so she

reached up and pulled her out. When Beth placed her on the ground, the cat took off toward the dogs and crawled in between them, snuggling closest to Gums. It surprised Beth that Kitty got close to the fire, but then again, she had the protection of her family this time around.

"Is that normal?"

"No, but they're an interesting bunch. I think they understand each other. They're different from the rest, and that gives them something in common. Gums has no teeth, Ozzy no tail, and Kitty ... well, she doesn't have much of anything left but the will to live."

She moved deeper into the room, really taking it in for the first time. The last time she was there, she arrived tipsy and left in the dark.

She walked toward the fireplace, which had a large wooden mantel, and ran her hand across the smooth surface until she came to a row of pictures. She picked up the first one and stared at Gray standing next to the President. She put it down and moved to the next one which showed him with Leonardo di Caprio.

"You hang with an interesting crowd."

He smiled. "Not really, but who wouldn't frame those?"

She couldn't blame him. She would have an I-love-me mantel, too, if she had pictures with notables.

"Can I get you a glass of wine or something?"

She'd kill for a glass of wine or a perfectly made old-fashioned, but those days were over ... at least for now.

"No thanks. I'm good." She stood in front of the fireplace until the chill lodged in her bones disap-peared. "Hey, about that night."

His phone rang, and his eyes grew large. He held up his hand. "I have to take this. You can take the second room on the right tonight." He rushed off and left her alone.

It seemed like the universe was working against her. Every time she tried to talk to him, something happened. She reached down and fluffed the fur of her pups.

"You ready for bed?" She was. The day had been emotionally and physically exhausting. Who knew growing a human could be so much work? "About a trillion million other women," she said out loud. She found Trip sitting on the kitchen table. After checking his water, she walked down the hall-way. The first door on the right was Gray's. She knew that from her one-night experience. She peeked inside the darkened room and got a whiff of his cologne. It was a unique blend of citrus and spice that made her want to sip lemonade naked between his sheets.

She inched down the hallway, finding a room on the left. A light shone from under the door, and Gray's deep voice seeped out from the pores of the wood. She could hear something that sounded like excitement, but she couldn't be sure because she couldn't make out the words. Afraid of being caught snooping, she dashed to the second room and entered. She expected to find something equivalent to a cot in the corner but was surprised to see a queen-sized bed covered in shades of gray. The painted walls weren't entirely white or gray. They were the color of a dove's wing.

The nightstand lights were lit, casting shadows around the room. A musician didn't decorate this room unless he kept that skill in the closet. Come to think about it, he looked like Jonathon and Drew Scott. Maybe he was a long, lost brother who went in a different direction.

The dogs followed her inside, but Kitty trailed behind. She was far more cautious of her surroundings.

"Don't get used to being here. I know it's far nicer than our house, but we're just on a sleepover and not even the fun kind. This one is only about sleep." She readied herself for bed and climbed between the soft sheets, feeling comfortable for the first time in weeks.

BETH WOKE to the smell of coffee. It was one of those smells that didn't sit right with her these days. She barely had enough time to scramble out of bed and get to the bathroom before the dry heaves took over.

"When will this end?" She flushed the toilet, pulled herself up from the floor by the edge of the sink, and looked at her ghostly white face in the mirror. "I hate mornings." That wasn't true. She hated the mornings when she was sick. She quelled that most days with dry crackers or peppermints but forgot to bring any along.

A knock at the door startled her.

"Just a second." She splashed water on her face and pinched her cheeks before she opened the door.

Gray stood before her in jeans and a T-shirt that was so snug it fit him like a second skin.

"Coffee is on the counter. Help yourself to whatever you need." He pivoted and walked down the hallway.

"Hey, can we talk?"

He peeked his head out his bedroom door. "I've

got to run into Copper Creek for a few things for my trip."

"Your trip?"

His smile widened. It was the kind of smile a person got when they opened a gift they'd wanted for a lifetime. "I've got an audition tomorrow in Los Angeles for a band called The Resistance."

"Seriously?" She knew the band. They were rising in the charts until their guitarist OD'd. They blew through several musicians, but the fit never seemed right. "I love that band ... or loved them before Taylor went and screwed it all up by dying."

He frowned and shook his head. "Dying screws up a lot of things." He stepped forward and looked at her more closely. "You okay? You look kind of pale."

Her heart took off, and she was sure a swarm of bees rushed into her belly.

"I'm fine." She had to come up with an excuse for why she looked like she'd just tossed her cookies. "I'm always pale when I wake up." She wanted to palm-slap her forehead. That was the lamest thing she'd ever said. "What I mean is, I've got a lot on my mind, and I'm stressed." At least that was the truth.

He frowned. "You need anything in Copper Creek?"

"Can you pick me up a furnace on the cheap?"

"I don't think they sell them at Target or Walmart."

"Then I'm good, I guess. Let me get dressed, and I'll be on my way." The dogs raced past her toward the door. Kitty stretched in the hallway like she didn't have a care in the world. "After I let them out."

She took a few steps toward the door.

"Call Wes Covington. He's the guy who helped organize this one." He shook his head. "Well, he didn't, but he has a crew, and I'm sure he can help you with whatever you need to get your place in shape." She moved toward the door. "By the way, nice jammies."

She looked down at her Hello Kitty pajamas. They were designed for a kid but came in all sizes. The rainbows, stars, and white kitties on their pink background always brought a smile to her face. "Thanks, I think." She was sure he was sarcastic, but whatever. He probably slept in plaid boxers and a white T-shirt with pit stains. Nothing sexy about that.

THE SUN SHONE BRIGHTLY, reflecting on the white melting snow. There was a crisp cleanness in the air that came right after the snow. It was like the heavens had purified the atmosphere. Small rivers of water were running down her driveway to the street. She was grateful for the warmer weather. At least she wouldn't have to freeze to death waiting for Wes to arrive.

She called him before she left Gray's, and he told her he'd be right over. Everyone's right over was subjective. Did his I'll-be-right-over mean after breakfast? Right over after I watch the news? Or, I'm heading out the door now, and I'll be right over?

She turned the handle to her door and took a step inside. "What the hell?"

Her shoes sloshed through several inches of water. Gums rushed inside to frolic in it like she'd given him a gift. Ozzy backed away. Kitty burrowed deeper into her chest.

"Where is all this water coming from?"

"Broken pipe," she heard from behind her.

Her hand went straight to her chest, nearly slapping Kitty upside the head. "You scared me." She now recognized Wes. He was Lydia's husband. She knew Lydia because she was at the hospital when Merrick got shot.

"Sorry about that." He moved straight to the closet that held all her nightmares and pulled a red lever up. "Frozen pipes are always a mess."

"How did a pipe freeze?" But she knew exactly; it was more rhetorical than anything else. What she was asking was how could this happen to her? Didn't she have enough going on that she didn't need another problem on top of it?

He glanced around. "You leave that window open all night?"

Her breath caught. She had left the window open, and she hated to admit it, so she stayed silent.

Wes walked through the water and closed it. "No matter because without a heater, they would have frozen, anyway. Anytime you have a hard freeze, you need to leave the cabinets open or let the water drip or keep your house warm enough to keep the water from freezing and bursting the pipes." He looked around her house and took in a big breath. "You won't be able to stay here. I need to bring in a pump to get the water out and then some industrial-sized fans to dry everything so you don't have a mold problem." He walked around the perimeter of her living room. "You'll need drywall repairs, the pipe replaced, and then we still need to address the furnace." He stomped on the wooden floor, sending splashes of water in every direction. "I'm not sure about the floor. It's going to warp and crack when it dries. Might be cheaper to tear it out and start fresh."

If she weren't standing in a shallow lake, she would have fallen to her knees. "How much is this going to cost?"

Wes chewed his lip. "It won't be cheap. What's your budget? I'll work within that."

Her laugh sounded like a cackle. "Budget? I have six hundred and twenty-three dollars to my name."

Both of Wes's brows shot up and nearly touched his hair. "What about credit?"

She didn't believe in it. Her mother had taught her and Merrick that if you couldn't pay cash, you couldn't afford it.

"I don't have any."

He cocked his head to the side. "As in yours is bad, or you haven't established credit yet."

"The second one."

"Wow, I'm shocked. Most people are up to their earlobes in debt before they finish college."

"I'm a cash-and-carry girl."

"Let me do some checking around. I'll put some feelers out and see what I can come up with. Maybe I can find a used furnace. First things first, though, and that's the pipe." He took another look in the utility closet. "The place is uninhabitable for a while."

A knock sounded at her door. She rushed to open it and found Gray standing there. "I thought you left."

"So did I, but then I realized I left my wallet on my dresser. And when I got back, I saw Wes's truck and thought I'd see what he had to say." He stared down at the water. "Uh-oh. It looks like a pipe burst." He scrubbed his palm over his face. "I should have thought about that before I brought you to my house."

"Your house?" Wes asked.

She almost forgot Wes was there. Gray seemed to take up a room wherever he was, which made her forget about everyone present.

"It's a long story, but, the furnace quit, the fireplace backed up, and my fish died, so Gray rescued us."

"Knight in shining armor, huh?" Wes smiled.

"No." Gray shook his head. "Just one night, as in she slept in the spare room. Not a knight as in white steed and castle and forever."

She was so tired of hearing him remind everyone that he was off the table. "Yes, we get it loud and clear. You're not available, approachable, or anything that might require any effort on your part. Got it. You're a one-night man, not a hundred-nights kind of guy." She turned to Wes. "You were saying?"

"You'll need to find someplace to stay for at least the next week, maybe more. What about your brother's house?"

She shook her head. "Nope. Deanna is allergic to cats. That's why I bought this place."

"Maybe the bed-and-breakfast?"

She let out an exaggerated breath. "No, Sage is ready to pop. No guests allowed."

She hated to admit it, but maybe she'd have to go back home. "Give me a minute." She pulled her phone from her pocket and dialed her mom.

"Hey, honey," her mother answered. "Can I call you back in a few? I'm packing up the rest of your things so the new renter can move in."

She couldn't believe her ears. "You rented my apartment?"

"You bought a house. Why wouldn't I?"

"Because I might have a flood and a fire and a bunch of other problems that could make my house uninhabitable."

"Welcome to home ownership, honey. Can I call you later?"

Beth hung up without saying goodbye. "Looks like I'm staying put."

"You can't. It's unsafe, it's going to freeze again tonight, and I can't do anything about the heater until I find one you can afford."

"So, basically I'd be better off living in my car." Both dogs were now on the couch, trying to avoid the water. Without it continually running, it hadn't risen any more since she arrived, but it hadn't dissipated much either.

Gray took his keys from his pocket and removed

one. "Here," he said and held it out. "I'll be in Los Angeles for a few days, anyway."

She shook her head. "No, I couldn't."

Wes moved forward and snatched the key from Gray. "You'll have to unless you want to live in your car."

Gray nodded to Wes, "I got to go," he said before he stepped toward the door and looked her way. "You should stay. I mean, the place looks better with a dog in front of the fireplace."

Wes laughed. "Yep, I bet that's the reason you offered."

Gray mumbled something about borrowing trouble before he left.

"Okay, then. You'll get together with Gray, and I'll figure something out with the house." He moved to exit like he was on fire.

"No, no, no, I'm not getting anything together with Gray."

Wes turned around to face her. "You'd have to be blind not to see that you guys have something sparking between you."

"You're wrong."

He shrugged. "How long will you lie to yourself?"

That was the question of the day. How long would she lie to herself and keep the truth from Gray?

CHAPTER TEN

He'd been gone a week and wondered if his house had survived Beth and her fur family.

"Hey, man, are you with me?" Bryson asked.

Gray refocused his attention back to the lead singer of The Resistance. "Yep, all here."

"Good, because when we go on the road, I need you to be one hundred percent present. Taylor was all over the place, and we don't have time for the bullshit that comes with a drug problem, alcohol abuse, family issues, or plain old stupidity."

This was a golden opportunity for him, but he couldn't help when his mind wandered from time to time.

"You don't have to worry about drugs, alcohol, or women. I've got no need for any of them. As for stupidity, I can't lie. I have my moments, but so does everyone."

"Sure enough," Bryson said. "Let's see how we sound together on the new piece I wrote." Bryson handed him the sheet of music. It didn't escape his attention that he didn't give any of the other members music. To Gray, that meant the song wasn't necessarily new, but it would be new to him. The other members had it down. This was a test. He hoped his last test.

"Let's do it." He grabbed his guitar and strummed a few chords before waiting for the drummer to lead them in.

It was hard to walk into a performance not knowing anything about the music, but he understood why Bryson did it. If they chose him for the band, he'd have to deal with many things they threw at him.

There would be another relocation. He'd keep the house in Aspen Cove so he could come and record with Indigo if they still wanted him, but he'd have to get a place in Los Angeles too. He used to have a place in Redondo Beach until Samantha asked them all to move to Colorado.

His life had been one change after another this last year, but staying busy kept his mind off other things.

He leaned in to see the chord progression. He

was one of those musicians who had to see things only once for it to be burned into his memory. It wasn't a photographic type thing, but muscle memory. He saw it; he played it; he knew it.

He liked the way the song changed time and how the pace slowed down, then picked up. It felt kind of like his life.

When the music ended, he looked at the rest of the band. They all stared at him like he'd turned the sea red.

"What?"

"No one has been able to play that yet."

Gray shrugged. "I guess you can't say that anymore."

Bryson chuckled. "I guess we can't. It's not a straightforward piece with all the time changes and chord progression."

Gray looked down at the music. While he knew there were difficult elements, it didn't seem all that tough.

"I've played worse." He thought of his words. "I'm not saying the song is bad. What I meant was I've played more difficult pieces." As the other members packed up, he did the same by removing his guitar and setting it in his case. "What now?"

Bryson rubbed his chin. "We've got a few more auditions, but I'd say you're at the top of the list."

"Great." He had hoped to have a solid offer by

the time he went back to Aspen Cove. "I look forward to hearing from you." He closed his case, shook hands with all the members, and walked out the door. He felt like he had the job in the bag until he met up with Jericho Waters at the studio entrance. There was only one guitarist he felt could take this win away from him, and that was Jericho.

Once Somebody's Love disbanded, he'd been on everyone's must-have list.

"Hey, man," Jericho nodded from the hallway. "You up for this gig, too?"

Just his damn bad luck. Gray didn't want to let the uncertainty he felt show on his face. "Thought I'd toss in my hat to see what happens."

Jericho leaned his instrument against the wall and took a cigarette from his pocket, then lit it.

Gray stepped back. It was a dirty habit he hated. It also reminded him of Allison, who smoked like a chimney. He should have known she wasn't pregnant when she wouldn't give up the cancer sticks.

"They're a great band. Too bad about Taylor, but drugs will kill you." He blew out a puff of smoke that nearly took Gray out with it.

Gray pointed to the lit cigarette. "So will those." He turned his back to the door and pushed it open with his shoulder. "Good luck with the audition."

Jericho laughed. "It's not if they want me. It will come down to if I want them."

Gray watched the door close before he turned and walked toward his rental car. Jericho Waters was arrogant and self-assured, but what he said was true. Bryson might want him in the band badly, but it was Jericho who would choose.

As he got into the car, he thought about his choices. He seemed to let the world make them for him. The difference between him and Jericho was that Jericho ruled his world, and Gray let the world rule him. That would have to change.

Rather than go back to his hotel for another night, he picked up his clothes and headed to the airport to fly on standby. If he were lucky, he'd get on the one o'clock flight and be back in Aspen Cove by six.

———

THE BEST THING about having money was he had options, and flying first class was always his preference. With one seat left, he got on the one o'clock flight and took a puddle jumper from Denver to Copper Creek, where he'd left his car last week.

On his way back, he drove past Pete's Pets and thought of Beth. The woman was on his mind all the time, and he didn't understand why. The sex was amazing, but then again, what sex wasn't?

Maybe she simply intrigued him. She seemed to care for others more than she did for herself, and that was an anomaly in his business. She also didn't seem impressed by who he was or what he offered. She was in dire straits, and she still wanted nothing to do with him. That was just plain old weird.

He got about a block away from the pet store before he made a U-turn and headed back. The whole week he was away, he couldn't get the look of shock on Beth's face out of his mind. Tossing the water from the fishbowl onto the fire was a natural reaction. He never considered her beloved fish.

Once parked in front of Pete's, he went inside to look at the betta fish. He didn't know why they called them beta when they were obviously alphas all the way. Calling them fighting fish was a better choice since that's what they did when they came into contact with another. He wondered how they ever procreated.

"Can I help you?" the girl at the counter asked.

He knew the second she recognized him because her eyes grew wide and a smile the width of a suspension bridge stretched across her face.

"You're—"

"In a hurry," he said.

"Oh my God, I can't believe it's you."

"Betta fish?" He hated to be rude, but when she picked up her phone and started texting, he knew she would fill the shop with her friends in no time.

"Over here." The clerk, whose name on the tag was Marianne, linked her arm through his and led him down an aisle lined with tanks filled with colorful fish. At the endcap were plastic cups filled with the flowy finned fighters.

"Show me the one in the worst shape?"

She cocked her head. "Why?" She moved closer to him, so her breast touched his arm. He knew how that would go down. She'd tell the world he felt her boob even though the reality was she rubbed it on his arm.

The best way to handle a situation like this was to make him undesirable or unattainable. The last time he told some girl he had an STD, which he didn't, but thought it was a clever ploy to get her to stop hanging on him, she told the *National Enquirer*.

He tried the next best thing. "It's for my girlfriend. She likes the underdog." He smiled. "That's why she chose me. She has a savior complex."

After a long sigh, Marianne dropped her hand from his arm and stepped back. "This guy looks pretty bad." She pulled a cup from the back. It was a blue fish whose fins looked more like straggly hair. To make matters worse, he was missing an eye.

"What's wrong with it?"

Marianne looked around as if making sure no one could hear her. "He's the current champion." She leaned in. "When the store closes, my friends and I take bets. It's kind of the MMA fighting for fish."

That confession appalled him. "How old are you?"

Her broad smile came back. "I'm legal."

He swiped the cup from the shelf. "That's animal abuse."

She rolled her eyes. "It's a fish, who cares?"

He walked to the register. "Beth does." He said it with so much conviction because he knew it was true.

He paid for the fish, and just as he exited the store, a carload of girls pulled in front. He knew if he didn't get away, he'd be stuck signing autographs and playing nice when all he wanted was to get home. He ran straight to his car, climbed in, and sped from the parking lot, leaving four disappointed teens behind.

He wasn't usually a homebody, but knowing he wouldn't walk into an empty house had its appeal and drove him to reach his place more quickly.

Back in Aspen Cove, he parked in the driveway, grabbed his guitar, and then picked up the cup. All the way over, he tried to think of what she'd call the fish. The only thing he could come up with was Foo after the Foo Fighters.

When he entered the house, both dogs greeted him. "Hey, boys." He set his guitar against the wall and ruffled Gums' fur before giving Ozzy a pet on his noggin. Why hadn't he ever gotten a dog? They were far less trouble than a girlfriend. Their love was abundant, and their loyalty unmatched. They always forgave you and seemed genuinely excited to see you. He needed a dog, but then he remembered that dogs, like women, needed constant attention, and he didn't have time for that. If he ended up playing for The Resistance, he'd be on the road. The life of a musician wasn't ideal for permanence.

"Where's your mother?" He chuckled because that's exactly what Beth was to them. Although, Ozzy looked at her like she was his girl.

Both dogs took off toward the hallway like they knew exactly what he said. With the cup of fish in his hand, he followed them.

At her bedroom door, Gums let out a howl that hurt Gray's ears, and seconds later, a very naked Beth rushed from the room.

"What's wrong?" She looked down at the dog staring up at her. She squatted in front of Gums with her back to Gray, moving her hands all over the dog.

All Gray could do was stand there looking

dumbfounded, holding a half-dead fish. She was perfect. Her skin was flawless except for the mole on her right shoulder that looked like a crescent moon. Her figure was hourglass perfect. She was far from skinny but proportioned just right for his tastes.

He felt almost guilty for staring, but he couldn't help himself. Everything they shared came rushing back to him in that instant: the drinks, the bedroom, the pleasure.

An unexpected hum slipped from his lips, causing her to shoot to her feet and whip around to face him. He had to admit, the front view was just as appealing as the back.

Her mouth dropped open, and her hands came up to cover her beautiful breasts. That's when she realized the rest of her was bare. It was comical watching her try to cover everything, and when she couldn't, she growled.

"What the hell are you doing here, Gray?"

If he were acting like a gentleman, he would have turned away, but turning away from the sight of Beth still wet from the shower was impossible.

"I live here. This is my house."

She shook her head while she moved Gums to stand in front of her and scooped Ozzy into her arms.

"Right. Sorry." She shifted from foot to foot.

Her eyes went from his down to what he had in his hands. "What's that?"

He held up the cup. "I saw this guy and thought he needed you." He took a step forward, and her eyes grew bigger.

"You bought me a fish?"

Any other woman and he'd be in serious trouble, but Beth melted before him. To her, a handicapped fish was like buying her a five-carat diamond. Holy hell, some guy was going to hit the jackpot with her. The thought of that made his junk twitch, but it also made the acid rise in his gut. Some other man would have Beth, which meant he wouldn't.

"Well, I felt guilty for poaching him."

She hung her head. "In all fairness, he was already dead."

"Still, I wanted to make it right." He held out the cup. "You want to come and meet him?"

She took a step forward as if she couldn't help herself, but then stopped as if she just remembered she didn't have clothes on. "Um... let me get dressed."

He laughed. "It's not like I haven't seen you naked before, Beth." He lifted his brow as if waiting for her to refute the claim.

A blush colored her cheeks. "I know, but on

that day, I had a couple of old-fashioneds to numb my embarrassment."

He stepped forward. "You have absolutely nothing to feel embarrassed about. You are—"

"Going to get dressed."

Gums let out a single bark as if concurring with her decision before he walked into the bedroom, leaving Gray with a grade A view.

Beth squealed before she pivoted and rushed through the bedroom door.

He laughed all the way to the kitchen. Yep, coming home to a full house had its benefits.

CHAPTER ELEVEN

Beth fisted her hips and stared at Gums.

"Why would you howl like someone had hurt you? All you had to do was bark." The dog bobbed his head back and forth but looked repentant. That made her feel guilty for blaming him. She was the one who rushed into the hallway, naked as the day she was born.

She hadn't even considered what she might look like to Gray. He didn't seem to notice the slight rounding of her stomach. Then again, it wasn't much to see. Her baby was only a few inches long and weighed about an ounce. She could blame the slight weight gain on overindulgence of bar snacks, which she seemed to eat by the cupful when at work.

Thinking about work made her step it into gear. She had to be there in less than thirty minutes, so she yanked on a pair of jeans, coupled it with an oversized T-shirt, and slipped on her shoes. Walking down the hallway toward the kitchen, she wrapped her hair into a messy bun. There was no reason to put on makeup because she wasn't trying to impress anyone.

The closer she got to the kitchen, the more excited she became. Gray was home, and he brought her a fish. Who did that? A man who pays attention, and they were about as rare as a unicorn.

She found him in the kitchen cleaning out Mr. Spitz's bowl.

"Hey," she said from behind him.

"Hey, back." He looked down at the bowl. "I hope you don't mind, but I went into your house to get this." He held up the bowl.

"No, that's great."

He looked between the fish and bowl. "Do we just dump him inside and fill it with water?"

She gasped. "No, we have to let the water sit for at least twenty-four hours. Forty-eight would be better." She moved to the plastic cup. "Tell me about this fish."

He stood up taller. "I don't know his background or his family, but he seems okay. Found him at Pete's Pets on my way back."

"What were you doing at a pet store?"

He shrugged. "I don't know. It's like it was calling me, and I couldn't help myself."

"Oh, I know that voice," she said. "It goes something like 'Gray, come in here and save me.'"

"Yep, something like that."

She turned the cup around several times to get a good look at the miserable creature.

"Why this guy?"

"Because he needed a rescue." He poked at the cup. "Look at him. He's all scraggly and only has one eye. The girl said he's the MMA fighter of the shop. They take bets on him, and he always wins."

Her jaw fell open. "They used him like pit bulls and roosters for fighting?"

"I guess. Anyway, it didn't seem right, so I bought him. He may never get better, but at least he won't get worse. I know you'll treat him right." He leaned over next to her and peered into the cup. "Now you have to name him."

Immediate inspiration came to mind. "That's easy; he's Stevie Wonder."

Gray shook his head. "You crack me up."

"Well, I'm good for something." She took over filling the bowl with water and set it on the counter. "I hate to go, but I've got a shift at Bishop's. It's karaoke night, and you know how your fans get."

"Ah, right. Maybe I'll come over and give the band a hand."

"Why do you guys do it?" She moved around the kitchen and took her bag from the table and picked her coat up from the chair. She'd grown comfortable at his home.

"It's good PR, and it's a way to pay back our loyal fans." He chuckled. "It's also great for Red because he has a hard time sleeping alone."

She lifted a brow. "Yes, he uses the bar like his personal dating service. I think he'll be happier now that he has his wingman back." She considered what that might mean for her. What if Gray wanted to bring a woman home? It was his house, and ownership entitled him to do what he pleased, but thinking about it made her heart ache.

He shook his head. "I'm not like Red. I don't bring a strange woman home on the regular."

She quirked a brow and kept it up long enough for her forehead to ache. "Right."

"No, seriously, I don't bring home strays." Was that a blush she saw rise to his cheeks?

She tugged on her jacket and zipped it to her neck. "What would you call me?"

He looked down, and then when his eyes lifted, she saw them smile before his lips followed. "Best night I've had in a long time."

It was rude to roll her eyes, but she couldn't help it. Here she was, standing in front of one of the best guitar players in the world, and he was telling her she ranked somewhere in his life.

"You need to get out more."

"I get out plenty," he said.

She turned and walked toward the door. "I knew it."

"That's not what I meant," he called after her.

She opened the door. "But it's what you said."

He followed her outside and rushed to open her door. "What's the news with your house?"

Talk of her house gave her hives. Wes had been there all week trying to Band-Aid things together. It was a nightmare unfolding, one house repair at a time.

She climbed inside her Subaru and buckled up. "There's so much I have to tell you." And there was. She'd start with the house and then move on to something that went like, "Hey, Gray, you're going to be a daddy."

"I'll see you later at Bishop's," he said right before he closed her door and walked away.

BETH HAD GOTTEN USED to the grind at Bishop's. She knew from working only a week who were the good tippers and who were the troublemakers. Sadly, just then, the troublemakers walked into the bar. Most would assume it would be rude men, but not in this case. It was a group of women who reminded her of the Puget Debs from *An Officer and a Gentleman*, but instead of bagging a naval aviator, they wanted to snag a rock star.

As she moved toward the table, she felt a little ashamed to judge them. She wasn't much different. She went home with Gray for a night of bliss. The only difference was she wasn't trying to corner him into a marriage. It was never her intention to get pregnant and trap him into something he wasn't up for.

"Good evening," Beth said in her sweetest tone. "What can I get you?"

The blonde, who appeared to be the group leader, said, "Red's and Gray's phone numbers and a round of lemon drop martinis for all of us."

That seemed to be the standard line because she heard it last time they came. "I can definitely help you with the martinis, but you're on your own for the numbers."

One girl grabbed Beth's arm before she walked away. "Do you think Alex will be here?"

Beth turned and stared at the woman. Right in that second, she knew she'd also inherited her mother's librarian stare.

"Alex is married and expecting a child with his wife, Mercy. While he may be here, he's off-limits."

The blonde who ordered the drinks laughed. "No one is ever off-limits. Do you think these guys are faithful? Why do you think Gray is probably still paying alimony? There's no doubt in my mind he cheated, and his wife ran into the arms of the guy from Third World."

"Oh my God, right?" The brunette who had the hots for Alex bounced in her seat. "I heard she was pregnant, and he was furious that she'd tie him down with a kid. They got into a huge fight, and she lost the baby."

That bit of gossip felt like a punch to the gut, causing Beth to stumble back. "I'll be back with those drinks." She nearly ran from the table straight to the woman's restroom. She felt ill but wouldn't throw up. It wasn't that kind of feeling. It was more a dreadful heaviness that strangled her heart.

When the door handle shook, she knew she couldn't hide in there all day. She splashed her face with water and took a few calming breaths before she returned to the bar. Bitchiness tempted her to water down the martinis, if not for the guys' sake for the women drinking them. Too much alcohol led to poor choices and unexpected things like pregnancy and STDs.

"Here you go," Beth said as she placed the three glasses on the table, but none of the girls noticed she had even arrived because Gray had entered and right behind him was Red.

Looking at Red now made her wonder what she ever saw in him. He had that I'm-a-good-for-nothing-scoundrel look about him. He was straight out of a historical romance novel. The over-privileged rake that could never be tamed until the right girl came along, but sadly, Beth didn't think there would ever be a right girl for Red. He was a guy who didn't understand the concept of moderation. Just last week, he took all three girls home.

"You think Red wants to do it again?" The third girl asked.

Beth stomped her foot to gain their attention. "Here's some advice. These guys will only use you. They aren't putting a ring on your finger, and they don't do round two." She pointed to a few guys she'd seen working for Wes. The same guys were there yesterday fixing her frozen pipes only to find the metal corroded on most of them. "Now those guys are keepers. They'd come home to you every day and be grateful to find you there."

"Boring," the lead blonde said. "If I wanted common, I could find that in Silver Springs."

Yep, Puget Debs.

"Suit yourself." She turned and walked back to where Cannon pulled beers from the tap for the quickly filling bar.

"Bring this pitcher and four frosted mugs to Dalton's group at the pool table." He nodded toward Doc. "I'll take care of the old guy there."

She knew how that situation worked. Cannon played tic-tac-toe each night, and Doc always won his beer. She was almost certain Cannon lost on purpose to the old man who seemed to dish out as much wisdom as he did medical advice.

She delivered the pitcher and the mugs to the pool table next to the small stage where Gray helped Red set up the mics.

"Hey, Darlin', can I get a Bud?" Gray asked. If it wasn't his voice that made her knees want to buckle, it was his smile.

She nodded and headed back to the bar. "I need a Bud for Gray." She leaned against the bar and took a deep breath. Her hormones were all over the place. Over the past week, she cried over the stupidest stuff like cat food commercials, but right now, all she wanted to do was murder the three women staring at Gray. She knew she was ridiculous because she had no claim to him, but it didn't stop her from feeling territorial.

Doc stared at her. "When you coming in to see me?"

Her heart responded in a quickening beat. She wondered if the Doc saw something no one else could. Was he like the vet she used to work for? Dr. Elliot could glance at a dog and know immediately what was wrong with it based on a look at the animal's eyes and coat.

Her hands went to her hair and tucked the loose strands back into the bun.

"Is that a requirement for living here?" she attempted to play it cool and hoped she was reading too much into his comment.

He glanced behind him and took a slow sip of his beer. When he set his mug on the bar, he licked the foam from the bushy mustache on his upper lip.

"Nope, but just thought you might want to get things checked out. Get on some decent vitamins, etc."

The world fell away from her feet, and she stumbled forward, catching herself on the edge of the bar. She leaned toward him.

"How did you know?"

"Now listen here," he whispered. "I've been doing my job for decades longer than you've been around. I can see the glow. I notice changes that most wouldn't, like the strain you're already feeling in your back, which is poor posture, and you need to deal with that now because it will only get worse. I've also noticed how your nose scrunches when you open a whiskey bottle, but vodka doesn't bother you. You eat bowls of pub mix like they're the magical cure to an upset stomach."

"Am I that much of a giveaway?"

"Only to a trained eye." He reached over and set his hand on top of hers. "Come and see me. We'll get you taken care of."

She smiled at the old man. "No one knows."

He nodded. "Then they won't hear it from me."

She breezed by Cannon, grabbing Gray's beer and heading over to where he sat surrounded by a group of girls. It was more of a gaggle since they reminded her of a flock of noisy geese.

His expression was stoic until she showed up, and he gave her a warm smile.

"Thanks, love." He reached for the mug, and their fingers touched, taking the chill of the icy mug completely away. He looked up at her as if asking her to save him.

"I'll leave you to your harem." She didn't expect the words to come out so clipped. She sounded like a jealous girlfriend. She'd spent one glorious night with him, but he'd never be hers. The group surrounding him was proof of that. He'd always belong to them.

"Hey, wait."

She turned around and waved her hand in the

air. "I've got to work." Looking over her shoulder, she plastered on a fake smile. "Looks to me like you've got your night cut out for you. Choose wisely; they've got that white-picket-fence look in their eyes."

CHAPTER TWELVE

Despite the bevy of beautiful women clamoring to get his attention, he couldn't take his eyes off Beth. She moved around the room like a ribbon in the wind, always out of reach but not out of sight.

"You want to do a duet," the buxom blonde beside him asked. "We can sing together first."

He shook his head. "Sorry, outside of the band, I'm a solo act."

She cleared her throat and started her rendition of "One is the Loneliest Number."

He started in with his version that he called, "Two will kill your bank account."

"You're such a cynic," she purred while trying to climb onto his lap.

Gray's eyes went to the bar and found Beth

looking straight at him. He didn't know why he felt guilty getting all this attention from other women when Beth was around, but it felt like he was cheating, and he wasn't the cheating type.

Was it because she was staying at his house? He didn't know what triggered the feeling.

"Hey, love." He said to the woman climbing him like a tree. "You should set your eyes on Red. His standards are far lower than mine." As soon as the words came out of his mouth, even he was shocked. He'd never been what you'd call a bona fide asshole.

"You're too good for me?" she asked.

He shook his head. "Not at all. All I'm saying is I'm not looking for endless hookups and one-night stands."

Before he knew it, she was in his lap. "Me either. I want my forever, and I'm fairly certain it's you."

He peeled her from him and set her back in her seat. "Oh, yeah. My forever needs to know something about me, like what my favorite snack is, or what cologne I wear."

She leaned in to inhale him. "It's Polo," she said with a smile.

"Wrong," a familiar voice came from behind him. Beth's hand settled on his shoulder. "He wears a custom blend called Nuance, and it's a mix of citrus and sage. His favorite snack is Fritos corn chips." She moved to the side where he could see her. "I need to replace your stash. I've eaten all of them."

Laughter bubbled up from his gut. "All six bags?"

She shrugged. "One a night while you were gone."

The blonde followed their conversation like a bobblehead on a horizontal slant. Her head bounced from Beth to Gray to Beth again.

"You're with him?"

"I'm not with him." Beth rolled her pretty green eyes. "I'm just using him for housing and heat."

The blonde took in Beth's outfit and moved to her makeup-free face and frowned.

"She's a bit plain, don't you think?"

A squeak of indignation flew from Beth's mouth. "Outside of his Frito habit, Gray likes clean living from his solar panel run house to the organic veggies in the crisper. He's not into artificial flavors, colors, or women." Beth pivoted and walked away.

Gray's shoulders shook with laughter.

"Are you going to let her talk to me that way?"

He looked at the blonde, whose name he couldn't remember. "Yes, you're not mine to defend."

"She lives with you?"

He hadn't thought of it that way. In the most

basic form, Beth lived with him. She was indeed his escape when it came to scheming women. He'd used her with the pet store clerk, and against his better judgment, he'd use her now. But wasn't it Beth who just told the girl she was using him for housing and heat? In his mind, they could use each other.

"She lives with me. We have kids together. Ozzy is the cutest, but we just got Stevie, so we'll have to see how he does."

"You foster?" She looked at him like he had grown twelve eyes, all different colors.

He shook his head. "Oh no, with Beth, it's all or nothing. You're in it for life or until a fire burns it all down around you."

He watched her scoot her chair back like he'd revealed he was Ted Bundy incarnate. Had he known it would be this easy to dissuade the opposite sex, he'd have put a tree-hugging, animal-loving, whatever Beth was in his house as a decoy long ago. To test his theory on his newfound undesirability, he stood. "What about that duet?"

Blondie's lips curled. "Nah, you go ahead. I think I'll visit Red."

"You do that." He walked toward the bar and took the end chair next to Doc. "How are you doing?" he asked the old man.

"Finer than frog hair split seven ways." Doc

folded the napkin with a tic-tac-toe grid on it in half and then slipped it under his mug. "What about you?" Doc looked over his shoulder to the table of women looking their way. "Is that your fan club?"

"Not anymore."

"How do you feel about that?" Doc shifted on his stool to face Gray.

"Given that I chased them away, I'm feeling pretty good. Women are trouble, and I'm not in the market for trouble."

Doc lifted his beer and gulped the last drink. "You got to know how to pick a good one."

Beth walked over and put a fresh mug in front of Gray. "You need another, Doc?"

The old man looked at Gray. "Only if he's buying."

Gray nodded. "Whatever Doc wants is on me."

"Be careful what you say, son. If you offer too much, there's always someone willing to take advantage of it." Beth walked to the taps and pulled Doc a beer. She set it down and walked away. "The best kind of woman is one who has your best interests at heart. She knows what you need before you do." Doc eyed the beer in front of Gray, which made him wonder if Doc was getting at something.

"Oh, no. I'm zero for one. I'm in the once burned twice shy camp."

"You can't give up. That's like not eating another

apple your entire life if the first one you took a bite of was rotten. Not all apples are bad."

"Look around you." Gray stared at the group of women surrounding Red. They were all jockeying to be the flavor of the night. At one point in his career, he was no different, but having too many women was like eating too many sweets. After a while, they made your stomach ache.

"Oh, he's not the apple," Doc said. "He's the worm. If you have problems with the women in your life, it's because you've set the bar very low."

"I don't disagree. The problem is, I'm too trusting. I married a girl because she told me I knocked her up. I pledged all my forever's to her. It turns out all she was after was a world tour and access to my Amex card."

"As I said, you've set the bar too low." He nodded toward Beth. "That one there. What do you think of her?"

Gray frowned because he thought of her far too often. "She's a nice woman. She loves animals, but she seems to leap before she looks. She bought the house next to mine, and it's a mess. Uninhabitable at this point, so she's staying at my place." He knew that sounded wrong. Doc seemed to think he was a playboy, and he didn't want his reputation rubbing off on Beth. "I mean, she's got the spare room, and I've been gone all week auditioning for a new gig."

Doc sipped his beer. "The best gig I ever had was parenthood. You really can't top that. I mean, you help make a human, and how you raise that little person decides the fate of the universe."

"Seriously, you think one kid can change it all?"

Doc chuckled, "Son, open your eyes and your ears. Think about the notables of the world who changed the trajectory of human existence, starting with Christ, and then there's Martin Luther King, John F. Kennedy, Gandhi, Nelson Mandela. Look what Imelda Marcos did for women and shoes." Doc chuckled. "In all seriousness, you can make all the music you want, you can fly a rocket to space, maybe even find a cure for cancer, but the most important thing you'll ever do is have a child. And how you raise that child will determine the impact they make on the world."

"What if you don't want children? Does that mean my impact isn't valuable?" The conversation intrigued him.

"No, it means your parents raised you to impact the world. Your contribution to society stems from their commitment to you."

Gray disagreed. "Not so. Look at how many people abandon their kids, and yet, they turn out okay, anyway."

Doc rubbed his beard. "They didn't learn from

osmosis. There was someone who stepped in to parent that kid."

"Now you're muddying it all up."

"Nah, I guess I'm just an old man trying to make sense of the world, and the only thing that makes sense is what you bring it. Maybe your music is your child." He lifted his shoulders. "My greatest contribution is my daughter, Charlie. Without her, I'd be less."

Gray patted Doc on the back. He was having a reflective moment. "Well, I'm never having any children. My career isn't one that's conducive to happy family life."

"We all make our choices. Just make sure yours doesn't set you up to be old and gray and lonely."

With that, Doc guzzled his beer and slid off his stool. "Time for me to go. It's *Dancing with the Stars* night. I want to see that football player win." He moved toward the door and exited.

The music started, and Red and the blonde took the stage.

"Looks like you've been traded in." Beth stared at the stage. "I probably shouldn't have spoken for you, but honestly, she's a gold digger."

"Well, if you fish from a pond that only has big-mouth trout, that's all you're going to catch."

Beth eyed him. "You've been hanging out with Doc too long. Now you sound like him."

Gray reflected on what she said, and Beth was right. It sounded like a Doc-ism for sure. "All I'm saying is if you're trolling for something different from a gold-digger, then it's probably best to fish from another pond." He waved his arms around as if taking in the entire bar. "This isn't about us. It's about the brand."

Red and the blonde belted out a poor rendition of "Love Will Keep Us Together," but Red was no Captain, and blondie didn't make a believable Tennille.

"Tell that to them. They seem to think it's all about them."

"That's because they're both delusional. Honestly, she's perfect for Red. He believes the sun rises and sets on his ass, and at this exact moment, so does she. By morning, he'll move on, and she'll have to if she wants to fulfill her dream of tour buses and band members."

Beth frowned. "Well, maybe he's simply a bucket list item, and once he's checked off her list, she's done."

The pain of that statement hurt his heart, or was that his ego? It wasn't often that a woman loved him and left him. They always seemed to want more, but not Beth. Maybe that was his attraction to her. Could it be that he wanted her simply because she didn't seem to want him?

CHAPTER THIRTEEN

Money pit was the best way to describe Beth's house. She fixed the waterline, but the rusty pipes were a problem. Her electricity was still wired from the forties, and Wes told her that the house probably wasn't grounded as far as he could tell. Her living room floor was warped and cracked, and each day she went inside to gather a change of clothes, she realized it would only get worse.

"Are you sure you can't fix the heater?" Beth asked Wes.

He shook his head. He'd been doing a lot of that lately. It had been two weeks since she'd moved into Gray's house. The first week was lonely and off-putting because she was on her own in her baby-daddy's place, but at least she didn't face the constant temptation of having him around. The second week he seemed to hang out at the bar. At first, she thought it was to hook up, but he never brought anyone home. Was that out of respect for her, or was he respecting himself? Gray seemed like a good guy, and he deserved more than a woman who used him.

Guilt ate at her because wasn't that what she'd done. Each time that thought came to the forefront of her mind, she tucked it away by telling herself that they used each other.

If the guilt of that wasn't enough to bother her, she still hadn't told him she was pregnant. It seemed whenever she opened her mouth to blurt it out, something stood in the way. She was a firm believer in paying attention to the signs around her, and what she was getting from them was now wasn't the time.

"I may have a lead on a slightly newer system. We're not talking this decade, but it won't cost you anything. I'm told I can have it if I haul it away."

Free was the very best word in her book. "Can I hire someone to do that?" Her heart picked up its pace. If she could get the furnace for next to free, she might be able to swing new pipes or electrical in a few months.

He leaned against the door and pulled his ringing phone from his pocket. He held up a finger.

"It's Lydia. Hold on a second." Wes turned from Beth, giving her the distinct impression he needed privacy. "Hey, babe."

She walked down the hallway into the living room. Every time she entered, it filled her with equal parts of sadness and joy. She almost cremated her fish in this room, but she'd made a few friends because of the disaster.

She bent over to touch the bottom of her sofa, relieved to find it had dried out completely. Then again, a wind tunnel was running through her home with the industrial-sized fans Wes had brought in. She had no idea how she'd ever repay his kindness. Up to this point, he hadn't charged her a thing. When she asked for his bill, he told her money wasn't the only currency in a small town. If she'd been anywhere else, she would have considered that a proposition, but she knew better. All she had to do was see Lydia and Wes together to know they were what she'd call soul mates. There seemed to be a lot of those around Aspen Cove, from Maisey and Ben to Katie and Bowie.

"Hey, sorry about that." He shrugged. "Apparently, there's a Thanksgiving potluck happening this Thursday at The Guild Creative Center, and I'm tasked with shopping."

Beth had seen the flyers going up around town and wondered if she should take part. She kind of had one foot in town and one foot out. She didn't consider herself a resident, even though she owned a house. So far, she felt like a transient, moving from space to space. First her brother's house and then to hers for a day, and now she lived in Gray's home.

It used to be that when she thought of home, her mind went straight to the basement apartment of her mom's house, but even that was gone.

While her brother wasn't pleased she moved in with the guitarist, there were few options. It relieved him that she hadn't shacked up with Red.

"When one door closes, another opens," she whispered.

"What was that?"

"Just thinking about all the changes in my life. Nothing is constant."

He moved toward the door. "My mom always told me that the one thing I could count on was change." He opened the door and met a blast of cold wind. "I'll see what I can do about that heater. I'm sure you'd rather spend the holidays in your own home." He looked over his shoulder to Gray's house. "Although, his house is pretty awesome."

She nodded. His house was fantastic. "Do you make the home kits?" One of the nights she got off early, she watched a movie with Gray and while the power went off on the block because of a storm, his stayed on because he lived off the grid with his smart house.

"No," Wes said with a shake of his head. "That's the Cooper brothers, but I helped with the details like installing the floors, tile, etc. A nice home is all in the details."

She couldn't agree more. "A nice home has heat. Let me know how I can expedite the matter. Tips have been decent, and I can certainly put a little cash forward. I don't expect you to pro bono the whole process. I realize you have to eat and pay bills too."

He laughed. "Now that's an excellent point. If you want to help me out with something, I'd be grateful if you could whip up a dish that will feed at least twenty for the potluck." Some sound that was a cross between a grunt and a growl came from his mouth. "Cooking isn't in Lydia's wheelhouse. It seems to be a family deficiency with the Nichols women, and I don't have the time to get to Copper Creek to buy whatever I need for some disgusting sounding green bean casserole, so if you could do that, I'll call us even for the heater pick up and install."

Beth's jaw dropped open. "Are you serious? You want a green bean casserole in exchange for heat?" She wanted to jump into the air, but she whooped and did a little victory dance. "I'll make you the best green bean casserole ever."

"It just has to be edible and not kill anyone." He turned and walked out the door. "See you Thursday."

Feeling a wealth of vitality, she skipped all the way back to Gray's house. She found him standing in his kitchen wearing nothing but a pair of flannel pajama pants and pouring a cup of coffee.

"You want one?" He held up the pot.

"No, I don't drink coffee." She'd told him on numerous occasions she didn't do caffeine. It was a lie, but a convenient one.

"I don't know how you can get through a day without the stuff."

She didn't either because there was a time she would have mainlined it with an IV into her system.

"It's not good for you."

He quirked a brow. "But a box of Red Vines a day is?"

"It's got gelatin in it, and that's good for your hair and nails." She gave him an argue-that-point look.

He filled the instant tea kettle and flipped the switch on. "Mint or Jasmine?"

She continued to stare at him until he cleared his throat.

"Oh, um. I'll take Jasmine." She loved the scent and the flavor. As the days progressed, she'd been feeling less nauseous but found that Jasmine tea had a calming effect on both mind and body. Now, if she could find a cure for her increasing libido, she was sure it was a pregnancy-related thing, but what if it was a Gray-related thing? Was he turning into her next craving like Red Vines and Little Debbie snacks?

"How's the house coming along?"

She was grateful for the diversion from where her mind and eyes kept wandering—Gray's body.

She cleared her head as much as possible and considered his question. Was this the day where he'd tell her she'd overstayed her welcome? She did her best to stay out of his way by going directly to her room after her shift and making herself scarce if he was home during the day. Most of the time, she sequestered the animals in her room and visited Deanna for a few hours before she came home to get ready for work.

"I should be out of your hair by next week, I think. Wes found a heater that will work, and all it costs me is a green bean casserole."

"You got suckered into the Thanksgiving potluck too?" He plopped a tea bag into a mug and filled it with boiling water. When he turned around and leaned against the counter, all she saw was muscle. She eyed him like a scientist looking at a discovery.

She took the tea he offered and leaned against the doorjamb. "Umm, I'm not going. I haven't been invited, but I can put together what Wes needs if that means I get heat." She chewed her lower lip until she was sure it was swelling. "I appreciate your hospitality, but having me here is putting some strain on your lifestyle."

He pushed off the counter. "You haven't been an issue at all." He walked to the table and took a seat. To her disappointment, part of his torso was hidden by the dark walnut furniture. "Contrary to popular belief, I'm not accustomed to taking stray girl's home. I told you that."

The way he used the word stray should have offended her, but she had a thing for the disenfranchised. Maybe that was why Gray attracted her. He didn't fall into any firm category. He was surrounded by people but seemingly alone. He had money but didn't flaunt it. He was handsome but didn't seem to know it. Gray was different, and that never bothered her.

"Tell that to the woman I found camping on the front lawn this morning." The term camping wasn't an exaggeration. When Beth left the house to walk next door, she found a woman crawling out of a tent pitched in Gray's yard.

"Are you serious?" He shoved his chair out and stomped to the door. As soon as his hand hit the knob, he stopped and stared down at what he wore. "Maybe I should put a shirt on?"

She turned so she could watch him. "Because you'll get cold, or you're afraid of her reaction?"

He frowned. "Both." He moved toward his bedroom and came out a few minutes later completely dressed.

"I'll be back in a few minutes. If you're going to Copper Creek, I wouldn't mind a ride-along. I have to make some kind of dessert for the potluck. Maybe you can help me figure something out."

"Sure, why not? Who knew my culinary skills would get me heat and a place to stay?"

"I didn't invite you to stay because of your culinary skills." He looked at her with fire in his eyes. It wasn't the heat she was referring to, but steamy hot regardless.

"You know, we need to talk."

He nodded toward the door. "No time for chitchat. I've got a trespasser to boot, and you've got to get dressed. We can grab a bite to eat in Copper Creek."

He turned on his heel and walked out the door. She considered standing at the window and watching him, but she hated the thought of seeing a woman's dreams get dashed. The poor girl was about to find out that Gray wasn't forever material. If he couldn't pay attention long enough for her to get the words I'm pregnant out, there was no way he could do long-term and committed.

The universe or fate or whatever was working against her. She'd go with it for now. If she knew anything about life, it was that it had its own time-line and forcing something to happen out of sync was like trying to put a square peg in a round hole.

One day it would all come together. That's what she told herself as she got dressed. There was one pressing question that kept bouncing around her brain. Why did she continue to lie to herself?

CHAPTER FOURTEEN

Gray briefly glanced at Beth. "What am I making?" he asked as he drove toward Copper Creek.

"What about pumpkin pie?"

He made a low throaty growling sound. "It's Thanksgiving, and everyone assigned to dessert will bring pie."

She shifted in her seat to face him. "What if everyone thinks like you and you have no pumpkin pie?"

"What are you bringing?"

"I told you, I'm not invited."

Out of the corner of his eye, he saw her sink into her seat and lose at least two inches of height.

"Everyone is invited. It's a community event."

A thought came to him. "How about you bring pumpkin pie, and I'll make something else?"

Though he didn't see her do it, he knew she rolled her eyes. She did that a lot when he was around, but he liked that she felt comfortable enough in his presence to be herself. The one thing he hated was when women hid behind a facade.

"Fine, I'll pick up a pie for me if, in fact, I'm invited. And if I'm not, then I'll sit at home and eat it by myself while you're all enjoying turkey and stuffing and potatoes and gravy and pecan pie."

He flashed back to a memory at his grandma's house. "When I was a kid, my grandmother used to make these pecan pie bars. It was like shortbread on the bottom and the best part of the pecan pie on the top. I loved them. Do you think we can make those?"

She pulled her phone from her pocket. "I think we can do that." She held the phone up. "I found something that sounds similar. You're going to need lots of ingredients. Pecans aren't cheap, you know."

He chuckled. "You know I make decent money, right?" He chanced a glance and saw her staring at the screen of her phone. It wasn't even like he said anything about his wealth. Most of the women he knew would have had a pen in hand and ready to take notes on all his assets.

"It's not about what you make, but what you spend."

He hadn't thought of it that way but broke was broke no matter how big the pot was when it started.

"And you know about broke?"

She huffed, and he turned his head to catch the roll of her eyes.

"Yes, I don't do credit, and I just bought a money pit." She reached over and touched his arm. "While I love that you've been generous by sharing your house, I'm paying for a mortgage on a property I haven't really lived in." Her hand dropped from his arm. "Besides, like I already said, I'm fairly certain my presence is changing your sleeping habits."

He laughed. "You do snore."

She reached over and slugged him in the arm. "I do not."

He pulled into the parking lot of the grocery store on the edge of Copper Creek. "Yes, you do. You're like a freight train. I can hear you all the way into my room behind closed doors."

She unbuckled her seat belt and reached for the door handle. "Okay, I may snore a little, but it's Gums that sounds like a freight train. He's been like that ever since they pulled his teeth." She opened the door and climbed out. "Are you coming? You have to pay."

"I always do," he said as he exited the car and followed her into the store.

They made their way around the grocery store, picking up what they needed for the potluck. "What about pizza for dinner?"

"Are you asking me to cook dinner for you, too?" There was a smile on her face and a sparkle to her eyes.

"No, I'm asking if you want me to pick up a frozen pizza, and maybe we can veg out in front of the TV and munch on junk all night." He knew he shouldn't encourage anything with her. He wasn't looking for forever. Hell, he wasn't even looking past next week. For all he knew, he'd get the call from The Resistance and he'd need to bounce.

"We can get Dalton's take-and-bake anytime. How about we live on the edge and do something healthier, like stir-fry, or what about pasta and meatballs if you're hankering for Italian food?"

He rubbed his chin, thinking about his choices. "Hankering? Who says that?"

"My old boss. She was a country girl who rode horses, raised pigs, and hankered."

He stood tall and fisted his hips, taking a step forward, trying to swagger like a cowboy. He put his best John Wayne voice to work. "Easy there, pilgrim. Tell me, what are you hankering for? Green shit or pasta."

She stared at him like he'd grown a third head. Her hand came up to his forehead. "Are you feverish?"

He decided to give her a hard time. Beth was fun to tease. "I have been told I'm hot."

There went the eyes again. "You're not. I mean ... you're okay, but I wouldn't want a calendar of you for my wall." She breezed past him and made her way to the ethnic food aisle.

"I've seen your calendar. It's Australian fire-fighters without shirts."

She giggled but then stood tall and pasted on a serious expression. "It's puppies who just happen to be held by hot Australian firemen."

"Right." He stood beside her, looking at the jarred pasta sauce. "Italian then?"

"Sure," she said, picking up a jar of vodka sauce. "I've been on the no-carb left behind plan for weeks. Why stop now?"

"Indeed." He grabbed a package of spaghetti and a canister of parmesan cheese. "You up for garlic bread?"

"I'm in. Let's go back to the meat department to get hamburger for the meatballs."

As they made their way down the aisle, she tossed several jars of spices along with a container of breadcrumbs into the cart.

At the register, she insisted on paying for the

dinner-making supplies and the pumpkin pie, but he quickly handed the cashier his card.

The trip back was a little quieter than the one there. He focused on figuring out why he liked her so much, and she seemed to stare off into space as if she were someplace else.

"So," they said in unison.

He laughed. "You go first."

"I was wondering why you went by Gray when Deanna told me your name is Gary?"

"I lost a bet." It was that simple.

"You bet your name?"

He thought back to that day with Red. "The band was in Seattle. Red and I were at a bar when a hot chick came in."

"Oh, no. Bets and chicks never end well."

He shook his head. "Nope. Anyway, he said I couldn't bag her, and I said I could. He said if I failed, I had to change my name to a color. He wanted me to go by chartreuse, but we settled on Gray since it was close to Gary."

"So, you crashed and burned?"

"Oh yeah, big time. It wasn't that I couldn't get her into my room. She was happy to follow me upstairs, but when the clothes hit the ground, it turned out Jamie was Jimmie. Red knew it all along, and he set me up."

What started as a snicker turned into a full-blown belly laugh. "Oh my God. What did you do?"

"What could I do? I told him he was far too beautiful, and I was unworthy. I dressed and headed down to the bar where I pulled up name change forms. Everyone thinks I changed my name because Gary doesn't sound cool, but I'm not about to correct them." He pulled into the driveway in front of his house.

"I can't believe Red made you go through with it."

"A bet is a bet. I'm sure I could have refused, but I'm a man of my word. I said I'd do it, and I did. In truth, Gray is a pretty cool name. It's gotten me a lot of ..." Hanging out with Beth was as comfortable as hanging out with the guys, but she didn't need to hear about his sexual escapades when she was one of them. "Dates. I've gotten a lot of dates with this name."

She reached into the back seat and pulled out a bag. "Yeah, sure. That's what you meant."

The dogs and the cat were waiting inside the door when he walked in. Their presence made his house feel like home.

"You feed Stevie Wonder today?" he asked. Each time he thought about her pets' names, he wanted to laugh.

"Yes, but I'm not sure he noticed."

"Ha, you're so funny."

She tossed him the head of garlic. "Start mincing, mister. If we plan to eat in this century, we should get things started. I like a sauce that simmers for a while, so the extra spices I add can soak in."

He moved beside her, and it felt so natural. While she prepped the sauce and made the meatballs, he went to work on the garlic bread. They moved around the kitchen like they were dancing together. She'd take two steps forward and he two back. They seemed in sync without trying.

Whenever she shuffled to the side to grab a spice from the cupboard, he stepped back and let her pass. After the first time, he gave her less room and found he liked the way her body slid against his.

Once she even stopped and leaned into him, but when he bent down to kiss her neck, she moved to the side and asked him if he was ready to eat.

"I thought we were going to let things simmer."

"Oh," she said, breathlessly. "Things are simmering just fine."

He opened a bottle of wine and offered her a glass, but she declined, saying that she was around booze all the time and liked to take a break. He poured himself a glass and joined her at the table for dinner.

It was the first actual meal he'd had there. He

took most of his meals at Maisey's, so this was a nice treat.

"This is amazing."

She twirled the pasta on her fork and took a bite. When she hummed in satisfaction, his whole body responded. He remembered that sound she made. It came from somewhere deep inside her, like her entire body was enjoying the experience.

"You need to stop doing that?"

She smiled. "Doing what?"

He stared at her. "That sound you make when you're fully satisfied."

Her left brow lifted while her right stayed in place. He didn't know why, but it was damn sexy. Hell, everything about her was sexy. He loved the way each time she moved in front of him, she left behind the scent of the tropics. She was coconut and mango and those pretty little flowers they put in Hawaiian leis.

"And you know that sound?"

He put down his fork and licked his lips, savoring the memory of her and that sound in his bed.

"I pulled that sound out of you several times that night."

With a deadpan face, she said, "Really? I don't remember."

"Need a refresher?"

He watched a blush rise from her chest to her neck and cheeks.

"Is that wise?"

"Probably not, but it sounds like fun." He stabbed a meatball and took a bite.

"Gray? Can I ask a question?"

He eyed her with skepticism. "You can ask, but I reserve the right not to answer." He found out a long time ago that most questions were self-serving. Although as soon as the words were out, he felt terrible because Beth hadn't asked him for anything. She was at his home because he insisted, not because she asked.

"You're such a lone wolf. Why is that?"

He rocked his head back and forth while he thought about her question. "It's not that I enjoy being alone. It's that I find most people aren't forthcoming about their motives."

"So, you've been burned before, and now you're afraid of the heat?"

He chuckled as he spun the spaghetti on his fork.

"Oh, I love the heat part. It's the chilling off I don't care much for. That cold icy feeling when things go to shit."

She cut her meatball into quarters and took a bite. She stared at him the entire time she chewed. He could see her mind working behind those beautiful eyes, but he wasn't sure what she was thinking. "Deanna mentioned you were married, but she didn't give details."

He took a deep breath and exhaled. "Were is the keyword."

"Right," she took another bite but kept looking at him as if she expected him to continue. He wasn't giving her his entire life story. Beth had that Hallmark look about her, and he was more of a Lifetime Original tale.

"Here's the short version. She trapped me with 'I'm pregnant' and then went after everything I had."

She dropped her fork. "Oh. You have a child?"

He shook his head. "No, and I'm not willing to say any more."

Beth nodded. She stared at her food for a few seconds more before she picked up her plate and tossed what was left into the disposal.

"I think I'm going to lie down for a bit."

"You okay?"

She smiled as if everything was right in the world, but he could tell it wasn't.

"Sure. Just tired. I guess the day has caught up with me." She attempted to clean up the kitchen, but he could see she was done. Whether it was with him or dinner, he couldn't be sure.

He moved toward her and pulled her into his

arms. "Look, I'm sorry. My life is a mess, everything is uncertain, and I'm not willing to share it with anyone right now."

She pulled away from him. "When did you get the impression that I wanted to be a part of your life?" She backed away. "Not everyone is like your ex. Not everyone wants something from you." She was halfway to the door when she stopped. "Not every person who's nice to you has a motive. Stop projecting your shit on me. As soon as my heater is in, I'll be out of your hair and your life." She pivoted and stomped out of the kitchen.

As he packed up the leftovers, he thought about her statement. It could be true, but it wasn't his experience. Was he so jaded he couldn't see a diamond amidst the coal? Was Beth that diamond?

CHAPTER FIFTEEN

Beth felt guilty for her ugly outburst and went out of her way to do nice things for Gray. She knew her behavior was a mix of hormones and disappointment. It seemed as if each time she had an opportunity to tell him the predicament she was in, everything came crashing down on her. Now that she knew the truth about his ex, there was no way she was telling him she was pregnant. At least not anytime soon. While he didn't go into details, all she knew was that the woman was pregnant and he didn't have a child.

Did he make her end the pregnancy? Did they lose the baby like the groupies at Bishop's said? It all felt so sad to her, and while she wished she had more information, she would not pick at what was a deep wound for Gray.

It wasn't as if she wanted him to jump aboard the daddy train. It would be great if he did, but she was prepared to do it on her own. This was a time when she needed her mom.

She flopped on her bed and dialed. The phone rang three times before she heard her mother's voice.

"Hello?"

"Hey, Mom."

"Oh honey, I'm so glad you called."

"I miss you."

"I'm coming for Thanksgiving. I hear you're having a potluck, and everyone is invited."

"We are. I'm making pumpkin pie."

"There should be a lot of that." There was a moment of silence. "Your brother asked me to bring his favorite stuffing. You know how he is about his Thanksgiving dinner. Do you have any requests?"

Tears pooled in her eyes and dripped down her cheeks. As if the dogs felt her emotions, they snuggled next to her and licked the salty tears that ran down her cheeks.

"I need a hug and some of those cheesy biscuits you make with Bisquick and cheddar."

"Cravings?" Her mother asked.

Beth hadn't paid much attention to what she

ate. She just had what she wanted, but in hindsight, she ate a lot of dairy and wondered if she was calcium deficient. She once heard women craved what their bodies needed.

"Mostly your cheddar biscuits and your hugs."

"I'll bring both with me tomorrow."

Beth felt a renewed sense of purpose. She'd stayed in her room since her dinner with Gray. He'd stayed mostly away from the house. Her phone vibrated with another incoming call, and she pulled it from her ear to look at the screen.

"Mom, I've got to go. I think my house might be ready for me again." She hung up and answered Wes's call.

"Hey, Wes." She crossed her fingers and held her breath.

"I'm at your place with the new heater." He cleared his throat. "I mean the new, old heater. I should have it installed and ready to go in a few hours."

She let out the breath she held. "That's amazing. I'll be right over. I can put your green bean casserole together while you get me hooked up." She hung up and tossed her clothes into a bag. She rushed around, straightening the room like her ass was on fire. She was sad she'd be leaving Gray's because she enjoyed his company when they were hanging out. He was different than she imagined.

He wasn't the player she once believed him to be. In fact, in a fit of jealousy, she followed him out of the bar one night when he walked out with a girl. She was sure he was bringing her home. Lurking around the corner, she watched him put her into a cab and tell her to set higher standards for herself. What man does that? That girl was climbing him like he was a ladder. She was a sure thing, and he passed it up.

Maybe her lousy luck brought her something good. No woman wants to have some asshole's demon spawn. Gray was a good guy deep inside, and if he wasn't dead set on staying single, maybe they could have worked out.

Looking down at her menagerie, she considered her situation. While she might not be with Gray, there was no reason they couldn't be friends. Hopefully, one day soon, she'd get the chance and the courage to tell him he helped bring her child into this world. And if he wanted to be a part of his or her life, that was even better. But she'd never force anything on the man.

"You guys ready to go home?"

Kitty, Gums, and Ozzy cocked their heads. She had shifted them around so much in the last few weeks, Beth wasn't sure they knew what the word meant. Trip and Stevie Wonder couldn't care less.

As long as she fed them, they were good. The fur babies were far more complicated.

She made her bed and gave the room a last glance before she walked out. Yep, she would miss being there with Gray.

She entered her home to find Wes and Baxter heave-hoing a large metal unit down the hallway.

"This thing is a beast," Baxter said. She didn't know him well but met him at the bar this week along with his girl, artist Sosie Grant. Aspen Cove seemed to be a haven for creatives.

"As long as it works, I don't care," Beth called out. A heater for a green bean casserole was the best deal she ever negotiated, and since Wes came up with the idea, it was the best deal she never negotiated.

She went back to Gray's house to leave a thank you note and pick up the fixin's for the casserole and Gray's pecan bars. When she returned, she got straight to work. She only had a few hours before her shift and wanted to get it all done so she could come home and enjoy her warm house.

And as lovely as that sounded, there was an ache in her chest like she'd lost something by returning here.

Two hours later, she smelled the heat seep through the registers of her house. It carried with it dust and whatever burned around the coils, but it smelled like heaven. Or maybe that was Gray's community dish that sat golden brown and delicious looking on her counter.

She wrapped the foil around the top of Wes's and Gray's dishes and set them on the table.

"Are you confident my house won't burn down if I leave, Wes?"

"You're good to go," he said. "I think this thing will last you another ten years, but I'd still recommend changing it out. The newer systems are more efficient and will save you money in the long run."

She looked past Wes to Baxter, who was packing up the tools. "What do I owe you?"

He shook his head. "I'm a blessed man. I can't hope for anything more than what I've got. I'm part of the welcome wagon."

On the outside, she smiled, but inside, the green monster grew. Jealousy had never been her thing, but everyone seemed to have what she wanted when she looked around her. They had love in their lives and people they could call their own.

She followed the two men to the front door and shut it once they left. When she turned around, she took in her home. It wasn't exactly what she dreamed of. At thirty-two, she thought her life would be something different, but what she had and where she was, wasn't that bad. She had a place of her own, three pets who loved her, and a fish and hamster who needed her.

Her hand fell to her stomach. She was going to be a mom, and while she didn't agree with her mother all the time, Elsa Buchanan didn't raise any bank robbers and serial killers. And that was saying something.

Seeing it was getting close to her shift, she rushed into her room and pulled out her fat jeans, which had now become her skinny jeans, and the black off-the-shoulder tunic that covered a multitude of problems, including the little tummy she noticed but nobody else did. She took her over-the-counter prenatal vitamins and grabbed her bag.

When she got to the door, she called to her babies, who lined up in front of her.

"Behave yourselves and no parties."

She didn't wait for the cock of their heads that she knew would come. She walked outside and climbed into her car. As she pulled out, Gray pulled in.

He smiled and waved, and Beth wondered if he'd miss her as much as she would him?

CHAPTER SIXTEEN

He hated he had missed her before her shift, but the recordings they worked on took longer than he expected. Mostly because Red kept whining about everything from the weather to the sound tech who was fifteen minutes late.

As he walked to the front door, he reveled in the pleasant thought that even though Beth was gone, the dogs and cat would be there for him. He'd grown accustomed to the joy that having a woman and animals brought to his house. Beth wasn't warming his bed, but she warmed his heart each time she left dinner in the refrigerator with a note on how to heat it. Her Crock-Pot pot roast was the best he'd ever had. He also liked the way everything seemed cozier with her there. It could be that she cranked up the heat to seventy every day, but he imagined it was more than that.

Beth was a thoughtful guest. She made sure she kept his space tidy and even defaulted to movie choices like *Spiderman* and *Terminator* when he asked what she wanted to watch.

He opened the door, expecting to find Gums and Ozzy waiting, but they weren't.

"Hey, guys, I'm here." He moved inside and shut the door behind him. When the dogs didn't run out of Beth's room, he was sure she'd locked them inside, so he moved down the hallway. "I'm coming to rescue you," he said.

At Beth's bedroom door, he turned the knob and opened it. Finding her bed neatly made and everything looking like she'd never been there made his heart trip. It somersaulted twice before it felt like it landed in the pit of his stomach.

He tried to tell himself it was because he'd miss the dogs and the cat, but he knew better. He liked how she seemed so genuine and selfless. He hadn't ever met a girl like that, especially since he became famous. Not wanting to open his heart out of fear, he had kept her at a distance. Now, as he was finally starting to let his walls down, she was gone. Or was she? He went to check dresser drawers and then the closet only to find them empty.

"She must have gotten that heater." He had a

terrible thought that made him half laugh and half shudder. He considered sneaking into her home to sabotage the system just so he could get her to come back, but he refused to sacrifice another fish, and he couldn't bring the pets back or else she'd know.

As he slogged toward the kitchen, he realized it was for the best. He wasn't planning to stay year-round, and he didn't do forever, so leading Beth on and making her believe he wanted more would be cruel.

When he got to the kitchen, he found a note propped up next to the coffeepot. It was on light-blue stationery and had his name written in pretty script on the front.

He slid a finger under the partially connected flap and opened it. The sheet of paper inside read:

Gray,

I can't thank you enough for your kindness. You stepped in when you didn't have to, and that means so much to me. I'm grateful I got to know the person you are, not the playboy guitarist I thought you were. I'm sorry about last night. I was moody and unreasonable. Hoping I didn't put too much of a damper on your love life. I want to be your friend. By the way, I made your pecan dessert. Stop by and pick it up before the event.

With love,

Beth

Seeing Beth and love on the same page did something to him. It had been a long time since he associated any woman besides his mother with the word love, and even then, that relationship was a love/hate thing. He loved his mother but hated that she still thought she had a say in his life. Then again, she'd brought him into this world, and that afforded her some privileges.

"She was right," he said out loud. "She told me Allison was a gold-digging whore."

She had manipulated everything so it benefited her. In the end, that wasn't her fault. It was his because he fell for it.

When his stomach growled, he looked inside the refrigerator and found a container with a yellow sticky note on it that had a smiley face.

Even though she was gone, she was still there. He warmed up the leftover pot roast and potatoes and sat in front of the television. It seemed like a waste of time. How many episodes of *Breaking Bad* could a guy watch? How many *Jeopardy* questions could he answer?

He rolled to his feet and picked his keys up from the table. He'd go to Bishop's Brewhouse. Two things were calling him there—an ice-cold beer and Beth.

IT WAS WEDNESDAY NIGHT, and the bar was hopping even though karaoke night was canceled due to the holiday tomorrow. Everyone was getting their merry on a day early. At the pool table were Dalton's friends. They were a bunch of badass bikers that stopped by often. To the average person, they looked like criminals with their tats and leather cuts, but they were nice enough. While he wouldn't want to meet up with any of them in a dark alleyway when they were pissed, they seemed like pretty decent guys.

With Doc at the bar and his girlfriend, Agatha, sitting next to him, the regular crowd was present. Doc was a cross between Wilford Brimley and Emmett Brown from *Back to the Future*. Agatha was the spitting image of Rose from *The Golden Girls*, though he imagined she had more of a Dorothy persona.

In the corner was Katie with Cannon. On her lap bounced Sahara. She had to be getting close to three because he'd seen her throw the temper tantrums kids that age threw when they didn't get what they wanted, but Katie and Bowie both handled it well. Then again, hearing their story and how Katie wasn't supposed to have kids and what a miracle Sahara was, he could see why she was spoiled.

He moved across the room toward the bar. Out of the backroom came Beth, carrying several bottles of spirits.

"Hey you," she said. Her smile lit up the room. "Miss me already?"

The truth was, he really did miss her. Especially their banter. With Beth, he could be himself.

"Yep, I thought about ways to sabotage your heater but couldn't do that to Stevie Wonder."

She poured him his favorite beer without him asking and slid it across the worn wooden bar top. "This one is on me."

"Hey now," Doc said. "If you're buying beer, I'll have another."

She waved him off with a swipe of her hand. "He gets one because he let me sleep at his house."

Doc chuckled. "I would have let you sleepover too, but Lovey already hogs the covers." Agatha reached over and cuffed Doc upside the head. *Yep, he's whipped.* Even men older than dirt fell to womanly wiles. Men were weak, and women were their freaking Kryptonite.

"You two complement each other." Agatha's cheeks pinked, and Gray was certain it wasn't from the wine. "I'm pretty sure you didn't get much sleep."

Beth's head was shaking before Gray could process a complete thought. "No, no, no," she said, "There was no monkey business going on at his house."

He lowered his head and mumbled, "Not this time, anyway." When he looked up, he caught her eyes, and they stared at each other for a moment. Was that interest he saw there? He'd caught glimpses of it here and there but wasn't entirely sure. His radar was broken and hadn't been repaired since Allison walked out.

"I can assure you, all we did was sleep and eat."

Doc emptied his mug and slid it to the edge. Agatha finished her wine and set her glass beside Doc's.

"Youth," Doc said. "It's wasted on the young." He slid off the stool. "Come on, Lovey, let's go home. I'm feeling frisky."

Agatha was two steps ahead of Doc when she got to the door.

Gray laughed. "Holy hell. I want to be him when I get ancient."

"You'll need an Agatha for that."

He sipped his beer. "Not my type."

"You have a type?"

He smiled. "I do. I like them intelligent, witty, and wonderful, and close to my age."

She wiped the bar off in front of her. "You're sapiosexual."

He nodded. "See, that's what I'm talking about. I don't even know what that means, but it's a turn-on."

As she always did, she rolled her eyes. "It means you like smart people."

I like you, though I shouldn't.

"Looks like it's going to be an early night." She looked out over the dwindling crowd. "Guess everyone has a pie to bake."

"Not me."

"Nope, you traded your bed for my sweets."

He nearly choked on his beer. "If we were truly trading my bed for your sweets, we'd still be between the sheets." He swiped at his forehead the way he did three-quarters of the way through a concert. Only then, he'd come away dripping in sweat.

"Stop flirting with me," she said.

"Stop compelling me to."

She walked around the bar to grab empties from the tables.

He watched the guys at the pool table eye her, and he didn't like it. Jealousy was unfamiliar to him. It felt like a guitar string being pulled tight around his stomach.

He glared at the oglers and moved around the

near-empty bar helping her pick up the abandoned mugs.

"What are you doing?" she asked.

"I'm helping. Do you get to close as soon as everyone is gone?"

She smiled. "Yep, Cannon is home with Sage. She isn't feeling all that great tonight, so he told me to lock it up when I wanted."

He walked to where the guys stood, racking the balls at the pool table, and pointed to his bare wrist as if he had on a watch. "It's closing time. Beth needs to get home to bake a pie."

The tall guy with the name Slider on his cut looked past Gray. "Is that right? You closing early, sweetheart?"

Beth's eyes grew large as she looked between him and them. "Umm, I was going to close up as soon as you were finished."

"We ain't finished." The guy lined up the rack and carefully removed it.

Gray wasn't ready to get his ass kicked, but he didn't want to sit in the bar all night. And with the way the guys were staring at Beth, he didn't want her there all alone either.

"Hey," he said to the guy who seemed in charge. He leaned in. "Look, if I pick up your tab, will you go?" He nodded over his shoulder toward Beth. "Help a guy out. I'm trying to get some pie." He knew if he put it that way, they'd be more amenable. It was kind of the bro-code. Thou shalt not block a guy's conquest.

Slider smiled. "You and her getting it on?"

"Not if you don't leave." Gray hoped they'd cut him some slack.

Slider looked his crew in the eyes and nodded toward the door. "Let's bounce."

They filed out of the bar in record time.

"Hey," Beth said, rushing to the door. "They didn't pay their tab."

"I told them if they left, I'd cover it."

"Why would you do that?"

He moved toward her. "Because it's Wednesday." He moved closer until their toes touched.

Her chest rose and fell with each breath. They seemed to shallow out and get quicker.

"You buy all drinks on Wednesdays?" It was a breathy question.

His hands rested on her shoulders, and her knees seemed to buckle, so she reached for his neck.

"Only when I want to kiss the bartender."

"You wha—"

He didn't wait for her to finish. Instead, he covered her mouth with his and licked the seam of her lips until she opened for him. When she sucked in a breath and let out a moan, it went straight into his mouth and fired up the passion he felt. He knew it wasn't smart to start something. He never doubled down. She'd spent weeks at his place, and nothing happened, but dammit if he couldn't stop kissing her now. Tasting like a summer breeze and smelling like the tropics, she was like a westwardly flowing wind on an exotic island. She was the umbrella on top of a Mai Tai. The umbrella wasn't necessary, but somehow it made things better.

When he pulled away, they were both breathing heavily. It relieved him that he wasn't the only one who felt that magnetic pull.

Her fingers came to her mouth. "Why did you kiss me?"

He couldn't tell her it was because he was jealous. "I wanted to. You enjoyed it, right?" If she told him no, he'd call her out. There was no way she'd kiss him like that if she didn't enjoy it.

"I did, but..."

"Look, I'm not putting a ring on your finger. It's just a kiss. There's no reason we can't, as adults, enjoy one another." He stepped back. "Now, let's get this tab paid and these mugs cleaned. I'm sure there's a Christmas movie on the Hallmark Channel we can watch."

She tossed the wet towel at him. "You're such a girl."

He shook his head. "No, but I like them."

"Close enough."

It took her twenty minutes to shut the place down. He followed her to her car and tailed her home. Would he have to destroy his heater to gain her sympathy and get an invitation to a sleepover at her place?

CHAPTER SEVENTEEN

Beth looked in the rearview mirror and watched Gray's headlights reflect back. She could still feel the tingle his lips left behind. It was such a bad idea, but she couldn't help herself. There was something about him that kept drawing her in. It was more than the fact she was having his baby, or maybe it wasn't. Did pregnancy mess up everything? Her hormones were all askew. One minute she'd laugh, and the next, she'd cry. Her boobs were bigger than they'd ever been. Those were changes she expected, but this was something else. She felt like one half to a whole. She was milk, and Gray was the cookie. He was the bacon to her eggs, and she knew she was in trouble when it came to him.

She pulled her car into the driveway and stepped out just as he parked.

"I'll be right over."

She opened her mouth to tell him she was tired and was heading straight to bed, but it was just after eight, and he'd see the lights on in her house if she lied.

"I'll get the hot cocoa ready." She wanted to slap herself for her mouth's betrayal. Her mind was screaming, *idiot*, while her body was saying, *get ready*.

"Be right back."

As soon as he disappeared inside his house, she ran to hers. Beth was greeted by her pets, who stared at her as if to ask, "where have you been?" They looked at her with judgmental eyes, like they knew what was about to happen.

"Don't you judge me." She pointed at Ozzy. "I've seen you humping Gums leg. I don't want to hear it." She let them outside and rushed to her room. What did a woman wear to a date that wasn't a date? Did she put on her penguin pj's and bunny slippers and pretend the kiss didn't move her to feel something? Did she play it casual and stay in her work clothes? Did she move into what she knew was a sure thing and change into something sexy?

When the knock sounded at the door, her choices were over. She looked in the mirror and groaned. She looked just like she felt, a tired barmaid with no sense of fashion and less self-control.

She opened the door to find Gray standing there looking like Adonis in his low-slung sweats and a T-shirt she was sure was a size too small.

"Though I'd get comfy."

She was about to comment with a sarcastic, Mmm-hmm, but heard Ozzy bark at the back door.

"Make yourself at home. I need to let the beasts in." She moved through the living room to the kitchen and to the back door. Along the way, she took several cleansing breaths to get all the carnal thoughts out of her head. Maybe the kiss was a fluke, and he was here to drink hot chocolate and watch Hallmark.

Usually, all three animals circled her when she got home, but today only the dogs were at her feet. Trip's cage was on the counter, and he stood on his back legs waiting for his treat. Even Stevie Wonder circled the top of his bowl. The only one missing was Kitty, who often stayed in bed. She couldn't be bothered with trivial things at night or when the temperature dropped below freezing.

Beth put two cups of water in the microwave and set the timer for three minutes while she searched the cupboard for hot cocoa. She had the powdered kind, which wasn't amazing but would do.

"I don't have whipped cream," she called out but didn't get a response.

As soon as the timer went off, she prepared the mugs and walked into the living room to find Gray sitting on her couch, scrolling through the channels. On his lap was Kitty. She had curled up and was sleeping.

"You made a friend."

He looked down and chuckled. "What can I say? The women love me."

Beth shook her head. "I know they do. They even camp outside your house to get a glimpse of you."

"Not anymore. I told them you were my girl-friend and an excellent marksman."

She narrowed her eyes and handed him a mug. "You didn't lie."

He stared at her for a moment. "About which part?"

"Obviously, I'm not your girlfriend."

He raised a fake rifle and aimed. "Then that means you're a regular Annie Oakley?"

"I'm more of the Sarah Connor type."

"Holy hell. I'll need to make sure I stay on your good side."

She plopped on the sofa, keeping the center cushion empty between them.

"Stop trying to steal the hearts of my animals."

He looked down at the sorry-looking cat in front of him. "How can I not love her? She's so pathetic looking." He slid his palm over Kitty's sweater.

"She's beautiful."

He set the cat to his side and moved closer to Beth. "You're beautiful." He grinned. "And a good kisser." He cleared his throat as he inched closer and leaned forward until his lips were at her ear. "What do I need to do to get between your sheets tonight?" He cupped her cheek and nipped at her lower lip. "I'll take a hammer to my solar panels, so I don't have heat, but I'd rather not."

At the mention of heat, a fire burned straight through Beth's skin. She knew she needed to come clean, but damn did he smell good, and his lips were little passionate pillows that left tingles everywhere they touched, and right now, they were on her neck and nibbling down.

There wasn't much room for thought because her body took over for her brain and her mouth. It was screaming *yes, yes, yes*, and they hadn't even gotten to the good stuff, and if her memory served her correctly, there was plenty of good stuff.

She pushed him away. Not to stop what was happening, but to stand and lead him to her room.

"Tonight, we enjoy each other, but tomorrow..." She let out a breath. "Tomorrow, we need to talk."

She was taking too long to get the fifteen feet

down the hallway to her room. "Fine," he said and swept her into his arms. "But tonight, we don't need words. All we need is each other."

He laid her on the bed and gently but efficiently undressed her. His hands roamed over her body, and she held her breath when his palm smoothed over her slightly rounded belly.

"I love a woman with curves," he growled. It was that low throaty sound that said he was about six seconds from being naked and inside her, and six seconds was too long. She knew she'd regret this tomorrow, but she'd enjoy it today.

"Stop talking and show me some action."

He stood and dropped his pants, and she once again saw what he offered. It was as good as she remembered.

He reached into his pocket and pulled out a condom. "I've got us this time. Last time I wasn't prepared. Thank God you were."

She swallowed hard. "About last time."

He rolled on the condom and climbed between her thighs. "Yeah."

Here he was all lined up, and she was about to experience nirvana once again. Did she ruin the moment and tell him, or did she accept the gift of his passion and deal with the consequences later?

"Too much talk and not enough action," she

said before she tugged at his hips, and he sank inside her.

He covered her mouth with his and silenced her words and thoughts. He spent endless minutes kissing her before he found a rhythm that drove her wild. The primal reaction took over, and nothing remained but the animalistic instinct to mate. He worshipped her breasts equally, taking his time to suckle and nip at each pink bud until her body vibrated beneath his.

When he closed his eyes and moaned, it was the sound of heaven. She was sure of it. He probably knew a hundred ways to drive a woman wild, but all she needed was the way he worked her body now. She was getting close. Her breath caught, and she held it until she fell over the edge. It started as a ripple and moved through every cell until her core squeezed him so tight he had no choice but to follow her to bliss.

The last thing she remembered was him kissing her forehead, and when she woke the next morning, he was gone, but every muscle in her body knew he'd been there.

CHAPTER EIGHTEEN

Gray turned on the shower and waited for the steam to fog his bathroom mirror. "What the hell was I thinking?"

He stepped inside and let the hot water rush over his body. At war with himself, he needed to wash this infatuation with Beth away. How many times did he have to tell himself that falling in love was a bad idea? Beth was a bad idea. But if she was a bad idea, why did it feel so right?

When he woke that morning, he found himself wrapped around her body, skin against skin, and everything about it was perfect. Lying there and holding her was all he wanted, but he knew better because to do so was suicide — absolute personal and emotional suicide.

He soaped his hands and ran them over his body, closing his eyes, remembering how it felt to have her fingers skim over his skin. Goosebumps rose across his body. Yep, he was losing his mind. He needed to get his head back in the game, back to a place where it was healthy for him.

After rinsing off, he dressed and walked into the kitchen to grab a cup of coffee. Normally, he'd set up a cup with a tea bag for Beth. She didn't drink caffeinated anything. The woman was a puzzle.

He shook his head. "Who doesn't drink coffee?" He considered boiling some water and delivering a cup of tea, but what good would that do? They weren't a couple. What were they? Neighbors with benefits?

He smiled. "I could do that."

He chugged down his coffee and stepped outside, only to find Beth's Subaru gone. He didn't know why it bothered him. He couldn't expect her to be there waiting for him. Hell, he'd snuck out of her house like he was a cat burglar, not making a sound as he tiptoed from her room with his shoes in hand, hoping the dogs didn't bark. They simply looked up from their bed and stared.

He climbed into his car and headed toward the Guild Creative Center. He figured if he'd have to be there in a few hours anyway for the Thanksgiving brunch, he might as well hang out at the studio and work on some material he'd been writing for a solo gig if nothing panned out with The Resistance.

The chassis creaked when the car thunked from the driveway apron to the street. The rise was too high, but he only noticed it when he left the house. It was like falling off a cliff and landing on granite.

Flakes of snow fell. First little flakes and then big white clumps drifted down from the gray sky. The weather in Colorado never ceased to amaze him. It was sunny one day and snowing the next. It could put down three feet in the morning, and a person was shoveling in shorts later that afternoon.

The short distance to The Guild Creative Center didn't take but a few minutes to get there, but in that time, at least a half of an inch of snow fell. Despite the inclement weather, several people were milling about the parking lot.

No sooner had he left the warmth of his vehicle than Doc Parker walked over to him. "Glad to see you, son. It's always nice when there's a lot of volunteers. Helps things get on faster." He raised his face to the sky. "This ain't lettin' up anytime soon, so the quicker we get unloaded, the less frostbite we'll have on our keisters." Doc pointed to the back of his Caribbean-blue 57 F-100 truck.

The only reason Gray knew what it was, was because his gramps had one just like it with sweet chrome bumpers and the nickname The Blue Goose.

Gray stared at the truck bed where folding tables at least a dozen high were stacked. "You want all those inside?" He hadn't planned on being manual labor today, but it didn't bother him. He was raised in a small town in Oklahoma where your neighbor wasn't only your friend but probably a relative, and you didn't have an option to say no to kin.

"You're a strapping lad, and I'm sure you can do it." Doc picked up two chairs that were left leaning against his tailgate and headed inside the center.

Just as he hefted one table from the bed, Red pulled up and climbed out of his truck. Gray always laughed at the Dually his bandmate drove and wondered if he was compensating for a little penis.

"Come and help me." He lifted the table and balanced the center on his head. "The faster this gets unloaded, the quicker they set up the food."

"No can do. I've got to restring my bass."

"That takes you minutes. Get over here and stop being an asshole."

Red grinned. "It's who I am."

"It's who you want people to think you are, and so you rise to the occasion. Don't forget that I've known you for years and I know your mom. If you don't bring your lazy ass over here, I'm going to call her and tell her your junk is about to fall off because you've had it in a hundred women this year."

Red laughed. "Dude, your numbers are skewed." He walked to the truck and picked up another table. "Don't call my mom. I'm already on her shit list because I'm not home for the holiday."

They moved toward the front door. "Why is that?"

Red made a throaty growl that sounded like a cat ready to barf up a hairball. "Going home is like an inquisition. All I hear for days is why I need a wife, and my mom needs grandbabies."

"She's got grandbabies." They set the tables against a nearby wall and went out to get the next load.

"I know. She had ten between my brothers' and sisters', but I guess grandbabies are like potato chips. You always need one more. What about you?"

"Same, man. All I hear about is my poor taste in women."

"Allison doesn't count. There are women, and then there are groupies. They aren't the same."

He had a point. Groupies were a different breed. There were the notchers who only wanted to check off a name on their to-do list, like the guys who put a notch in their belt for each conquest. Then there were the diggers who brought their shovels and bags to carry away your assets. It wasn't that either was terrible as long as you knew what you were getting. The problem with Allison was she acted like a notcher but concealed her tools. That was the one thing he couldn't stand: a woman with an agenda. Just be upfront. Honesty was always the best policy.

It took six trips in all to move the tables inside. When he and Red started toward the studio, Doc called them back.

"We're not done here, boys." He pointed to the longest wall where Maisey and Ben stood. "Go ask Maisey how she wants the buffet set up."

Red grunted. "Maybe I should have gone home." Despite the grumbling, he slogged toward the owner of the diner.

"Howdy boys," she said in her friendly, tip-me-well voice.

"Hey, Maisey," Red used his flirty voice that drove the women wild. By the blush to Maisey's cheeks, she wasn't immune. "Where do you want me?"

Ben stomped over. "Six feet under if you don't stop flirting with my wife, son."

Maisey giggled. "It's been a long time since anyone fought over me. I'd like to see who wins."

Ben blew her a kiss. "I'd win because I'm an angry old cuss. Now get those tables set up over here. You got twelve of them, so make a U with two, then eight, and then two. We'll set up a salad, main course, and a dessert section."

While they set up the food tables, Doc and Agatha placed the card tables for dining. By the looks of it, they were due for a large crowd.

Each job they finished only moved them on to the next job Doc had ready. The following two hours flew by. Before Gray knew it, the townsfolk showed up with steaming hot dishes, cold salads, and enough dessert to give the town diabetes.

With dessert on the brain, he thought of the pecan bars Beth made for him.

"I've got to go. My dessert is back at home." Beth's home, not his, but no one needed to know that.

The door opened, and Beth walked in carrying several dishes. "Looks to me as if your dessert just showed up. I think I should nibble on that sweetness."

"Careful man," Gray warned. He didn't like Red looking at his woman like she was on the menu. *His woman?* "She's not for you."

Red laughed. "Why, because she's yours?"

"No." Though that word came from his mouth, his body vibrated with a big resounding yes. Even his brain and heart screamed in the affirmative. One look at her, and he was back in junior high, rubbing up on a girl at the dance to get the thrill of a feel. She produced that addictive feeling, like having too much coffee, but despite it, he knew he'd reach for another cup. A shaky, uneasiness rushed through his veins. He was needy and wanted more. She was the more he craved.

He rushed over to her. "Let me help you." He reached for plates that seemed ready to topple.

"Uh-oh," she said as one tipped sideways in a scene straight out of a movie. They balanced, dropped, and dived until they both were nearly on the ground. Her purse spilled all over the floor, and they were both laughing but saved the desserts.

"Oh my God," she said on the end of a giggle. "I sacrificed my bag, and probably my self-respect." She yanked at her dress, which had ridden up to her hips, revealing a sexy pair of black panties. "But the desserts are fine."

Maisey rushed over. "Let me help with these." She swept the desserts up and layered them on her arm like the professional she was. Gray never understood how such a tiny woman could handle so much. He'd seen her arrive at a table in the diner with no less than ten plates lined up both arms. He felt like a wimp to have nearly dropped the three dishes he and Beth struggled to control.

"Thanks, Maisey." Beth scooped up the items

that had spilled from her purse. They both reached for a bottle, but he got there faster.

"Give me that," she said with a voice two octaves higher than usual.

She grabbed for the bottle as he lifted it and read Prenatal Vitamins. The container dropped from his hand like it had burned him.

Gray's jaw dropped.

"I can explain."

"If it's mine, you'll have to." His chest caved in like a thousand pounds of pressure had crushed his sternum. He thought she was different, but she was just another Allison, only this time the baby might be real.

"It's not what you think. I mean, it is. I'm pregnant," she whispered.

"And I bet the next thing you'll tell me is it's mine."

Her head fell forward. "It is."

The sinister sound of his chuckle chilled him. "Then it's exactly what I think, but it won't work. I'm not marrying you."

She swept the rest of her things into her bag and stood. "I never asked you to." She looked around and whispered, "I didn't expect this to happen."

He wanted to scream at the top of his lungs. "That's what they all say, sweetheart, but then you find out they poked holes in the condoms."

She gasped and stepped back. "I would never. That was my mom's doing. I didn't know."

He sucked in the pain of the verbal punch to his gut. "That's rich. I've never heard that one." Their conversation was gathering some attention as their voices rose. He wasn't the type to make a scene, even though he wanted to turn over every table in the place.

"You've got to believe me." She moved forward and reached out a hand to touch his arm.

He stepped back. "I'll need proof, and then, if the kid's mine, I'll write you a check." He shook his head. "I can't believe I fell for it twice." He turned and walked toward the door.

She rushed after him. "Where are you going?"

"It's none of your business. We aren't married."

She narrowed her eyes and glared at him. "Here's the thing, Gray." She said his name like it tasted bitter on her tongue. "I wouldn't marry you if you were the last man on earth, and I don't want a damn thing from you."

He pivoted and headed to his car. Stopping halfway, he spun around to face her again. "You'll get something from me because I'm not that guy, but those are the keywords. I'm not that guy ... *your guy*." He continued on toward his car and climbed in. He started it and let the engine rev, hoping the sound would mimic the rage he felt. But sitting next to the fury was another emotion he didn't expect, and that was fear because if she were truly pregnant with his child, he'd never walk away. He wouldn't be able to. Next to being the lead guitarist for The Resistance, being a father was the only thing he had ever wanted, but his line of work wasn't ideal for fatherhood or honest relationships.

He drove out of the parking lot and headed straight for the highway. There was no way he could stay in town right now. He needed space to move and time to think.

He turned on the radio and playing was The Resistance. The song was "Deceitful." The universe was telling him something. He needed to get out of Aspen Cove. He didn't have time to wait for the band to call him. He didn't care if it was a holiday or not, he was calling Bryson. This day was about being thankful, and he had little left to rejoice.

He dialed Bryson's number. Musicians never got a break, so he expected him to pick up, but it went to voicemail.

"Hey, man, it's Gray. I was checking in to see where you're at with the auditions. I'm tossing a few things around, but I wanted to give you first dibs. Let me know."

He hated how the lie tasted salty and bitter on his tongue. He hated how his happiness or lack thereof came down to a woman. He hated that he hated it all and wished it was different.

In his head, he heard Doc's voice. *Now listen here, son, you decide what your life will be like. Just make sure you're fair to everyone, including you.* It wasn't something Doc had ever said but sounded like something he would.

Was he being fair?

CHAPTER NINETEEN

Beth debated returning to the celebration or going home to cry. She was ninety percent leaning toward home, where there were fur babies to hug and console her. Nothing was going her way. She hated to borrow trouble, but that little voice in her head said, *What's next?*

"Beth," a familiar person called from behind, causing her shoulders to sag.

She knew better than to test the fates and spun around to face her mother.

"Hey, Mom." Part of her wanted to run to her mom and throw herself into her arms, but that would only prove that she couldn't handle adult problems. So, she bucked up her shoulders and put a smile on her face. A smile her mother would know was fake, but Elsa Buchanan wouldn't say a thing, or so she hoped because if she mentioned one word about the baby or the father, Beth wouldn't be able to control the watershed of tears destined to fall.

"You look well." Her mother's eyes rushed over her but settled on Beth's eyes.

"I'm good." She swallowed the lie, but it stuck in her throat. She tried several times to get it down. "I forgot you were coming," she choked out.

Her mother chuckled. "I doubt that, but you may have wished I wasn't."

Beth stared at her mother with caution. Was that a prediction or a promise? She never knew with their exchanges.

"Did you bring a dish?" Beth asked, hoping to turn the conversation somewhere that wouldn't make her want to weep.

Her mom spun around, making a perfect circle in the snow with her sensible shoes. "I brought enough to feed an army." Elsa opened the back of her SUV, and the aroma of a full Thanksgiving meal filled the air.

Usually, Beth would have breathed it in, but when the first hint hit her nose, her belly churned and lurched. She took off toward the tree line and made it to the edge before she lost what little she had eaten that morning.

Always having a weak stomach, it didn't surprise Beth that she was sick. Stress hit her in the gut and getting a double whammy of it with Gray's angry dismissal and her mother's presence would make a steel stomach quiver.

A hand patted and rubbed her back, and out of nowhere, a tissue showed up near her face. Beth stood and wiped her mouth.

"Thanks, Mom." She could no longer hold back her emotions and fell into her mom's arms and sobbed. "You were right."

Elsa laughed. "I usually am." She pulled Beth closer to her chest. "But it doesn't make me happy." A hand stroked her hair. It was a loving gesture that made Beth feel even worse for pushing her mother away. "I take it the guy who zoomed from the parking lot was the baby daddy?"

With a tear-streaked face, Beth stepped back and snorted out a laugh. The way her mother tried to sound hip and cool always cracked her up. Baby daddy was vernacular that didn't sound right coming from her librarian mother's mouth, but neither did the song "Apple Bottom Jeans," and her mother sang that non-stop for close to a year.

"It was. He just found out and feels betrayed because I didn't tell him sooner."

Her mother cocked her head. "Why didn't you?"

She took in a deep cold breath and let out a

mouthful of fog. "It's a long story. How about you come over to my house later and I'll tell you?" She set her hand on her stomach. "For now, let's get your contribution inside and feed your grandbaby."

Elsa nodded. "Okay, but I'm not letting you avoid this conversation for too long." She lifted out a box of casserole dishes and handed them to Beth before taking a similar box in her hands. "Let's go make merry."

Beth followed her mother inside the center where everyone gathered around while Elsa set out her famous sweet potato pie and the dressing her brother Merrick loved.

Red rushed over to flirt because he didn't have a soul or a conscience. She was never so grateful to have the wise counsel of Deanna and her brother when they told her to stay clear of him.

"Be careful, Mom, that one will have you hanging from the rafters dressed in only a smile."

"How would you know that?" Merrick asked. She hated the way he could slink up behind her. It was how he always got dirt on her when she was a kid. He moved like a cat—silently.

"Your wife, of course."

"I like the sound of that," Merrick said. "Wife is a good word."

Elsa reached over and cuffed him up the side of

the head. "Not every woman needs a husband." She
stared at Beth.

"No, but if you have one, he should be a good
one, and I want to be the best I can be for my wife
and child."

Elsa raised her hand into the air. "You're an
anomaly."

Red cleared his throat. "So, does this mean I
have a chance with your mom?" He whistled.
"Dude, she's a total MILF."

Merrick took a step forward. "You want to live
to eat dinner? If so, I suggest you walk away."

The clanging of silverware on a glass began, and
Doc stood on a chair in the center of the room.

"Can I have your attention?"

For an old geezer, Beth was shocked he could
stay on the chair or climb on it, for that matter. By
the way the Bishop brothers hovered nearby, they
were surprised too.

"I want to say thank you to Samantha and
Dalton for opening up The Guild Creative Center
for our community celebration. Aspen Cove has
grown over the last few years. Sometimes with
growth, there's pain like more traffic and differences
of opinions that drive wedges between neighbors,
but honestly, we're a unique community. We aren't
just friends or neighbors, we're family." He looked
around the room, and his eyes stopped on Red. "Ex-

cept you, son, you're something else, and I haven't figured it out yet, but you'll come around." He pointed to the tables that overflowed with food. "Enjoy a meal or two. Don't forget the pharmacy is well stocked with Tums and Pepto."

Sage raised her hand. "It's less stocked." She let out a little burp and covered her mouth. "I bought most of the Tums, but if you're in dire need, come to the B and B."

Doc smiled, "See, even Sage would share her stash with you. Not to hold up the feast, but I challenge you to find at least one thing you're thankful for and, as we always do, make sure you never meet a stranger in town. After the first hello, they become more." Bowie and Cannon helped the old man down, and everyone stood as if waiting to see who would dine first.

Sage shook her head. "If no one is going, I will. I'm eating for two." She grabbed a plate and loaded it up. Before long, happy eaters filled the tables.

As Beth looked around the room, her heart pinched. There was so much love here. Was it wrong for her to want a piece for herself?

"Hello," a voice came from her side, and a tall, slim older gentleman sat next to her mom. "I'm Lloyd, and you're beautiful?"

Beth sighed. Even her mother was attracting the attention that could lead to love. Was Beth destined to live her life alone? Was her soul mate a toothless shepherd or a tailless dachshund?

While her mother chatted with the man, Beth pulled out her phone and texted Gray.

Believe me or don't, but I can tell you at least a half dozen times I tried to let you know, and the universe thwarted me. Think about all the times I said, I need to tell you something, or we need to talk. Just saying. Before you think I've duped you, you need to reflect on our times together. As for wanting anything, I never did, so keep your checkbook locked away. I don't want a thing from you.

Before she chickened out, she pushed send.

For the next thirty minutes, the room filled with only soft murmurs as the crowd spent their time making a dent in the buffet that could feed hundreds.

A screech filled the air and all the chatter silenced in the room. Next to the dessert table was Sage, and she was standing in a puddle of water.

"It's time," she told Cannon. The poor man's face went ashen.

"It's time?" he asked.

Sage grabbed a chocolate chip cookie from the

counter and shuffled toward her sister Lydia. "You're up, sis. Contractions are three minutes apart."

"Jesus, Sage, why didn't you say anything?" Lydia grabbed her bag and rushed toward her sister. "You know better."

Sage grabbed her belly and groaned. "I wasn't missing dinner." She pointed at Lydia's husband, Wes. "I want a plate of leftovers. You'll take care of that, right?"

He hopped up and headed to the food table. "Got it."

When a groan left Sage's lips, Cannon swept her into his arms. "Time to have my baby."

She grimaced and cupped his cheek. "If I yell at you and tell you I hate you, it's probably true, but only in the minute, okay?"

"I love you."

She grabbed for her belly. "I'm starting to hate you."

"I'll always love you."

Cannon carried his wife out the door. Lydia followed close behind.

Doc yelled to her. "If you need me, let me know. I'll be here eating pumpkin pie."

"You ready, sweetheart?" her mom asked.

"Shouldn't we help clean up?"

Her mother smiled. "Oh, that nice man Lloyd

said he'd be happy to deliver our dishes later on tonight." Her mother slid her arm through Beth's. "Now let's get you figured out."

Beth climbed into her Subaru and waited for her mother to pull in behind her, and then she moved slowly through the snow to her house.

She prayed everything was in order. Mostly she prayed that she'd make it through the rest of the day without another crisis.

Once in her driveway, she waited for her mom to park, and she led her to the front door.

"It's not grand or anything but—"

"Don't make excuses, Elizabeth. Never be ashamed of who you are or what you have. And re-member that your children will see their lives through your eyes, make sure you show them the possibilities."

That choked Beth up. She turned the door handle and opened the door. "Welcome to my house." There was a sense of pride that filled her. This was truly her place, and no one could take it away from her.

"Oh, honey," her mother said as she walked in-side. "It's lovely."

Beth tried to see it through a parent's eyes and realized that it was probably a bittersweet feeling for her mother. A part of Beth knew that having her downstairs was a comfort, but she also realized that a parent's greatest joy should be seeing their children thrive.

Elsa walked around the living room, taking it all in. "You did well."

Beth shed her jacket and moved to the kitchen where she knew her pets would be waiting for food.

"I did terribly, but it all turned out well." She thought about Gray and how kind he'd been to let her stay. "When everything went to hell with the heater and the flood and Mr. Spitz dying, I wasn't sure I'd make it, but Gray helped pull me through."

"Gray?" Her mom's perfectly plucked brows lifted. "Who is Gray and what mother would give her son a name that's hardly even a color. At least that Red guy has some passion to his name."

Beth pointed to the chair by the table. "Have a seat, and I'll make us some tea." She put the kettle on and prepped the dogs and cat food while she waited. Once the water boiled, she made two cups of tea, fed the beasts, and sat down next to her mom.

"Gray is the baby daddy." She looked down at her stomach.

"I don't like him if he left you out in the cold and took off."

Beth shrugged. "You called it. He doesn't want

to create a forever with a one-night stand. Well, two nights, if we're honest."

"Two?"

Beth sighed. "Last night was amazing."

Elsa studied her. "Oh, you're in love with him."

With a wave of her hand, Beth dismissed the notion. "Oh please, what's love anyway?"

"It's what you're feeling for that man right now. I know the look. It's not like I haven't been in love before."

That came as a complete surprise.

"Who did you love?"

"Oh, honey, did you think yours or Merrick's father didn't mean a thing to me? I was head over heels in love with Merrick's dad, Marcus, but he wasn't the marrying kind. I thought I could change his mind, but even a pregnancy wasn't holding that man down."

"So, you poked holes in the condoms?"

Her mother frowned. "I like to romanticize it and say it wasn't my fault that my broach pin just happened to puncture a packet. It was only one packet, but we both know that's all it takes. Regardless, I got your brother, so the risk was worth the reward." She sipped her tea and looked past Beth. "As for you ... I was madly in love with your father. I thought he loved me. I thought many things like he was single, and he was honest, and he was a good man, but I was wrong. He was married, and he was a liar, and he wasn't a good man for me."

"Is that why you never talked about him?"

Elsa moved her chair closer and set her hand on top of Beth's. "Honey, you are not your father, and I never wanted you to think that because he wasn't good, you weren't. Your child will see the world through your lens until they're old enough to adopt their own vision. I wanted you to know how wonderful you were and that you came into this world to do great things. How you got here is irrelevant. That you got here is what's important."

Beth took in the words. Her mother was protecting her, and she had always done that. Yes, Elsa Buchanan was a pain in the ass, but she was a fearless mother—a lioness who'd rip out the throats of anyone who dared to threaten her family.

"I love you, Mom, and I'm sorry for how we left things."

Her mother smiled. "I'm not. In the process, look at how much you've grown. You've got your place. You're going to have a baby. It's all turning up roses."

"Thorns, maybe. I'm working on the roses."

Elsa chuckled. "Everyone starts somewhere. Now you start by telling me about this Gray guy."

Beth began with the story of his name. "You see,

his name was Gary, but he lost a bet and legally changed it to Gray."

"I don't know, Beth. All you have is your name, and he hasn't got his. What's the attraction?"

Beth pulled up the Indigo site and pointed him out. "It started with this."

Elsa took the phone and studied the picture. "Okay, so he's hot."

"Yes, but it's more than that. He's funny and kind, and after Mr. Spitz died, he rescued Stevie Wonder from a pet shop who bet on him like a prizefighter." She told her mom about Gray's ex and how each time she tried to tell him, something thwarted her attempt.

"I can see why he's gun shy. And you could have done better. There were probably a million opportunities you had and passed."

She couldn't deny it. She lived in his house for a while and could have blurted it out several times, but she wanted the timing to be right. "I guess there's never a right time to say, 'hey, you've got skilled swimmers, and they hit the target, you're going to be a daddy.'" She sipped her tea. "Then part of me wanted to be strong like you and prove I didn't need a man to make this work."

"Oh, honey, it's not about needing a man. It's okay to want one. No one ever needs a man, but they come in handy on trash day and grocery day."

"I like him, Mom. Well, I usually do, but I get to hate him a little today for thinking the worst of me."

Her mom leaned forward and hugged her. "All you need to do is to let him see the best of you. If he's worth keeping, he'll come around. If not, you'll be fine."

There was a tap at the door, and Elsa smiled. "I think that's our dishes."

"Are you flirting with that cowboy?"

Elsa giggled. "Oh, is he a cowboy? You know what they say … save a horse and ride a cowboy."

"How did he know my address?"

"I gave it to him."

"How did you know my address?" Beth had never told her, and divulging personal information, even if it was his sister's, wasn't in Merrick's lane, so her mother didn't get it from him.

"Oh, honey. I'm a mom. Do you think there's anything you do that I don't know about?" She kissed Beth's forehead. "I'll see you tomorrow, sweetheart."

Elsa was out the door before Beth could process that her mother had been in town less than a day and already had a date. Just when she thought she was alone, her mother peeked her head inside.

"I'm supposed to tell you that Sage had a boy."

"Thanks, Mom. See you tomorrow?" She hoped she would because she was a soon-to-be mother in need of her own mother right now. When it came to parenthood, Elsa Buchanan was always there for her kids. She was an excellent mother. In Beth's heart of hearts, she hoped she'd be as good of one as her mom. And the bigger question was, would Gray ever want to step into a father role? How could he if he thought she'd tricked him?

He needed to know everything, and so she picked up her phone and sent him a text. Once it was all out there, it was up to him what he wanted to do with the information.

CHAPTER TWENTY

Gray sat in the bar of the Marriott Hotel in downtown Denver, sipping an old-fashioned. He tried to drink something else, but nothing tasted quite so good. He knew it had nothing to do with the drink but the memory.

"Hey there," a buxom blonde said, sitting down next to him. "You look familiar. Do I know you?"

"Nope." He picked up his drink and took a sip. It tasted like Beth's lips the first time they kissed.

"Are you sure?"

He closed his eyes and took in two cleansing breaths. He should have had the drink delivered to his room.

"Look, you and I both know who I am." He glanced past her to where her friends were taking pictures of him with the woman. "I also know that whatever you think is going to happen isn't. I'm done with casual pickups. Done with women who feel a romp in the sheets puts a ring on their finger."

Her cherry red lips thinned. "Who in the hell wants that? And what makes you such a catch?" She slid off the stool onto her heels. "I might have considered sliding between the sheets, but not because I want anything from you. Welcome to the twenty-first century, asshole. Women don't need men. We've got batteries and sperm banks. Why would we put up with your bullshit when we don't have to?" She fisted her hips, accentuating her slim waist. "Yes, I knew who you were, but it had little bearing on me." She glanced over her shoulder at her friends. "For them, you're a big deal, but for me ... I've grown out of my puppy brains. You were alone and looked like you could use the company."

He gulped the rest of his drink down. "You're saying if I asked you to come up to my room, you wouldn't have?"

"No, because I don't sleep with assholes." She pivoted and walked away.

What the hell was happening in his world? Women flipping the script.

He paid his bill and headed to his room. In the hallway, a woman with cognac-colored hair walked in front of him, making his heart skip a beat. Had Beth tracked him down?

Had Red told Beth where he was staying? On any other day, he would have been angry, but the familiarity of her called to him.

He took a few quick steps forward and reached out to tap her shoulder.

"Beth?"

The women spun around with wide eyes. Eyes that weren't Beth's.

"Excuse me?" Her hand lay over her heart like he'd scared her.

"Sorry, I thought you were someone else."

She dropped her hand and smiled. "Lucky girl."

"Not really, I'm kind of an asshole."

"We all have our days." She turned and left him standing there.

He realized that maybe his ego had genuinely gotten in the way. Being a musician had its ups and downs, and perhaps the up of stardom was a down. Few people were authentic when they were around him. Most people were hired and therefore said whatever they thought he'd want to hear. The others were opportunists who went along for the ride. Beth was different. Hell, she didn't even give him the name most people used for her. She told him her name was Liz. That one unforgettable night, she didn't interrogate him about his assets or ask about upcoming tours. Nope, she asked the more profound questions like what music did for his soul. She asked him how it made him become a better person.

It hadn't. He was so used to having people take advantage of him that he'd lumped the whole of humanity together.

He turned back toward his room and entered. The last few days he'd spent in Denver made him take stock of his life. He filled the first with too much booze and fury. How could he have been so stupid to leave birth control up to her? While most men would continue to blame her, he couldn't.

The one thing he prided himself on was his ability to be insightful. After the marriage debacle, he'd become more self-aware, or at least tried to be. Sadly, Beth had proved that he wasn't as evolved as he hoped. He'd been acting like a knuckle dragger.

Her words played back in his head, *I wouldn't marry you if you were the last man on earth, and I don't want a damn thing from you.*

He would have had a hard time believing it, but he got a second dose of female independence today from blondie, who wasted no time in telling him that men were not a requirement.

He walked across the room and flopped onto the bed, and pulled his phone from his pocket. The best person to call when he had woman problems was a woman, so he dialed his mother.

It rang twice before she picked up. "Gary, is that you?"

"Hey, Mom. Don't forget it's Gray now." While the bet was stupid, he was never a fan of his name. It belonged to someone else, or so it always seemed.

"Don't you give me that. I named you Gary after your uncle, and you'll always be Gary to me. You can call yourself Twiddle Dee, but your name is Gary. Now tell me, what's up with you?"

He rolled to his side and looked out the window at the blue skyline.

"Why does anything have to be wrong?"

She sighed. He could almost see his mother's eyes roll. That's what she did when she made that sound.

"Gary, now you listen to me. I get the obligatory calls on major holidays and my birthday, but it's not like we have a Sunday chat date. Is this about a girl?"

He stayed quiet for a moment.

"You didn't even call me on Thanksgiving. You texted, which is a big red flag. Is it that Allison again?"

The mention of Allison made him want to laugh. With this new kink in the smooth ribbon of his life, she didn't even deserve any thought.

"No, Mom, but it is about a woman."

"I knew it."

He heard the chair scrape on the floor of the kitchen.

"I'm comfortable. Tell me you didn't knock someone up again."

He groaned. "Mom, Allison was never pregnant."

"Too bad, because that would have been the only good thing about that union. Now tell me about his girl. Will I like her?"

He hadn't even considered if his mother would like Beth, but the answer was an unequivocal yes. "You'd like her. She's kind and considerate, and she rescues animals."

"That's the first time you've ever talked about a woman and didn't lead with her looks."

"Oh, she's pretty, but not in the Hollywood glamorous way. She's real." Saying that out loud made it seem truer. "Here's the deal. Yes, she's pregnant, or at least says she is." He felt guilty putting it that way because he was certain Beth wouldn't lie to him.

"Lord almighty, Gary," she hollered. "You can afford condoms, can't you?"

It all came back to that. "Yes, Mom, but she had one. And according to her, she didn't know her mother had poked holes in it. What mother does that?"

His mom laughed. It wasn't a little titter but a full-blown bend over and grab her belly laugh.

"I'd say an idiot, but desperate times call for desperate measures. If it's true, then she wanted grandbabies."

Gray had received a long text from Beth that first night, but it was like overeating, and he needed time to digest and feel comfortable.

"That's what she said. Her mom was tired of waiting for her brother to give her grandkids, so she sabotaged their stash, and Beth took a packet from her brother's drawer."

"Aww, I like the name Beth. What about the brother?"

"He's expecting a child too."

"What you're telling me is this girl didn't trap you?"

"It would seem not, but what I'm telling you is she's pregnant. Also, she didn't tell me right away because she said we always got interrupted, but Mom, she was staying at my house for weeks after her heater was out."

"Hmm. Does this girl live in town?"

He chuckled. "She's my next-door neighbor."

"Oh, wow."

He couldn't believe how everything had turned

out. "It's a long story, but in summary, Beth is pregnant, and I don't understand why she didn't tell me right away."

"Honey, you don't blurt it out at dinner and say, 'pass the peas, and by the way, I'm pregnant.' Maybe she was waiting for the perfect moment."

"Or maybe she never intended to tell me." After their last face-to-face conversation, he wondered if she was ever going to tell him. Maybe she was telling the truth and wanted nothing to do with him or from him. That almost hurt worse than him thinking she trapped him. "She said as much when I left her in the parking lot."

Silence settled between them. The chair scraped the floor again.

"Do you love her?"

"Geez, Mom, how am I supposed to love her when I don't know her that well?"

"You need to read a romance book. Ever heard of love at first sight?"

"Sure, but I figured it was people thinking with their parts and not their brains."

His mother cleared her throat. "There's that, but after that moment, when your parts are happy, there's often nothing left. Tell me this. If she wasn't pregnant, would you want to see her again? Do you have enough chemistry to make something of the attraction?"

That's why he called his mom. She got straight to the core. The pregnancy didn't matter. It did, but it was a secondary player to the issue at hand. He might be in love with Beth.

"Oh, Mom. I like her, and that scares the hell out of me." Right there was the truth, and Mom always got it out of him whether she was trying to find out who broke the window or who ate the last Twinkie.

"Then go next door and talk to her. Even if things don't work out, you can be friends. The woman is pregnant, and it's most likely your child. She didn't ask you for anything. That says something about her and her motives."

"I'm in Denver. I ran."

His mother chuckled. "That's your MO and always has been. When things get tough, you run, but you always go back and fight. You picked up your guitar when your father died, and you ran, but it worked out so far. Maybe this is the universe's way of telling you it's time to stay."

He laid on his back and stared at the ceiling. For the first time in days, he felt calm and clear.

"You're right. I need to face this problem."

"You calling it a problem makes it one. Do me a favor and redirect your thoughts. When you see Beth, think of this as an opportunity."

"I will, and Mom?"

"Yes, baby?"

"I love you. You are always my rock and safe space."

"I love you too. When you two figure it out, I'd like to meet her."

"Okay." His heart skipped a beat. "But what if she wants nothing to do with me? What if I'm the last man on earth she wants?"

"Gary, you may be a runner, but you're not a quitter. Fight for what you want."

He hung up the phone and smiled. His mother was right. He wasn't a quitter, and tomorrow he'd let Beth see the fighter in him.

CHAPTER TWENTY-ONE

Why did the day have to evaporate like ice on a hot sidewalk? Beth spent it in Cross Creek picking up a few new clothes. Stuff that would hopefully fit her for the next few months. She looked at her watch. If she rushed home, she had time to love on the pups for a few minutes before she headed to work.

When she pulled into her driveway, her heart rate sped at the sight of Gray's car in his. He'd ghosted her since he left, which told her he wasn't the kind of guy she'd ever be able to count on. She hated to stereotype people, but musicians were known for their commitment to the craft, not women. Especially not women they thought tricked them.

She came clean and told him everything. It was

all she could do. As her mother would say, you made your bed, and now you have to sleep in it. She wished her mother had stayed longer because seeing Gray home made her need a hug.

She killed the engine and exited the SUV, grabbing the bags and taking them to the door.

"Hey," Gray said, stepping from his porch. "Let me help you with that."

She shook her head. "No need. I've got it." She rushed to her house and fumbled with the keys, trying to get them into the lock before he caught up to her. In her haste, she dropped them to the porch.

"Let me help you."

She inhaled and put on a fake smile. "I really can get it." She bent over and picked up the keys, but he took them from her hand. His touch made her entire body tingle.

"Please. Just let me help you."

She wanted to scream at him and ask if he'd done enough, but she couldn't blame her situation on him. She was in charge of her body and protecting it, and she failed.

"Thank you," she said as he inserted the key and unlocked the door.

The dogs were waiting on the other side. Gums wagged his tail while Ozzy wagged his bottom.

She breezed inside and went straight to her room to change for her shift. She couldn't wait to put the new pants on. Having to lie on her bed and force herself into her size tens was getting old.

His footsteps pounded up the hallway.

"Beth, we need to talk."

"Can't right now. I have to work." She turned around and found him leaning on her doorjamb. Gathering up the outfit she wanted to wear, she moved past him, brushing her shoulder against his chest. Each time she came into contact with him was like getting charged—like a shock directly to the heart.

She rushed into the bathroom, and he was right behind her, but she closed the door before he could enter.

"Come on, Beth. Don't shut me out."

Anger rippled across her skin.

"I'm not the one who took off for days. Forgive me while I recover from the whiplash."

"You can't hide from me forever. We're having a baby."

She tugged off her jeans and shirt and pulled on the roomier clothes before she flung the door open and pushed past him.

"No, I'm having a baby, and I don't need your contribution."

She stomped back into her bedroom and slipped on her shoes before grabbing her bag and keys and heading for the door.

"Just answer me one question. Why didn't you tell me right away?"

She stopped at the door and spun to face him. "I already texted you that answer, but to add to it, imagine how hard it would be to tell a man you're pregnant with his child when all you heard was how he never wanted any." She opened the door and looked back toward him. "Lock the door on your way out."

She ran to her car and climbed inside before she could have another run-in with Gray.

Five minutes later, she was at the bar filling pitchers, getting ready for karaoke night. It would be a busy night, and she was grateful for it. It would keep her mind off Gray as long as he didn't show up, and it was always a good tip night.

Cannon leaned against the bar like it was the only thing keeping him up.

"You look like hell," said Beth.

"Babies are hard. They don't sleep much."

Her hand came to her rounding tummy. She made an appointment with Doc and was going to have an ultrasound. Being a single mother wasn't the dream, but how many people got their dream?

"You should go home and rest or go into the stockroom and take a nap on that cot you have back there."

He looked around the bar. "I wish."

"Don't wish, just do. Goldie will be here at six, and we can handle it for a few hours. If it gets too crazy, I'll come and get you."

His tired eyes brightened. "Really?"

She pushed on his shoulder to get him to move. "Go, I've got your back."

Cannon disappeared into the stockroom, and the door opened, and the band walked in without Gray, which was a relief.

"You want a pitcher?" she asked Red. With Samantha and Deanna pregnant, Red and Griffen were the only drinkers besides Gray in the group.

"Yep, and the ladies will have club soda." He made a face. "It's a wonder any babies get born. Take out the alcohol, and life gets boring."

Samantha cuffed him upside the head. "I'm hormonal, so be careful what you say. I can still replace you."

Red placed a chaste kiss on Samantha's cheek. "Darlin', I'm irreplaceable."

"Assholes are a dime a dozen," Deanna added.

The door opened, and in walked Gray. "Speaking of assholes," Beth said as she brought over the beer and sparkling water.

"Your brother will be here in a few. He was on the phone with your mom. Is there something up?" Deanna lifted a brow.

"Can't imagine what." She turned around and

walked back to the bar. She'd taken the gag order off her mom because as the days went by, it would be harder for her to hide her pregnancy. At this point, there was no reason. The father knew, and that's all that mattered. She'd get around to telling everyone else in due time. She was still coming to terms with it herself.

Dalton's biker friends took their place by the pool table, and she delivered their pitchers. The next to enter was Goldie, who always had that just made love glow about her.

"Hey, girl. How's it hanging?"

"All good."

Goldie cocked her head to the side. "You got new clothes?"

Leave it to the fashionista to know what was hanging in everyone's closet.

"Just a few things. My pants were too tight."

Goldie laughed. "You got to lay off on the pub mix. It's all carbs and goes straight to the ass."

"I'll keep that in mind." She glanced at the table where Gray sat staring at her. She knew she should ask him what he wanted, but she needed as little contact with the man as possible. "Can you see what Gray wants?"

"Sure thing, doll, but by the way he's looking over here, I'd say he wants you."

She shook her head. "Oh, he definitely doesn't

want me."

"Girl," Goldie said, "I know men, and that look is the look of want."

"Just go get his order, please."

While Goldie got Gray's order, Beth moved around the bar's periphery, getting other's drink requests.

She was on her way back to the bar when the door opened, and in walked her brother. He scanned the room until his eyes fell on Red.

"You," he said, pointing at the bass player. "You're dead." He marched over to the table and picked Red up by the collar and punched him in the face before he dropped him to the floor.

Red scurried back. "What the hell, man? What was that for?"

"For knocking up my sister, and I'm not finished. You will do right by her."

The entire room went silent as everyone watched the drama unfold.

"I never touched your sister."

"Wrong answer, asshole." Merrick bent over to grab Red again, but Gray jumped in between the two.

"Move out of the way, Gray," Merrick growled.

"Can't. You're hitting the wrong man."

Beth stood there speechless. Half the room was staring at her brother, and the other half was staring at her. Goldie had her phone out, recording the entire episode that would no doubt be on *Getting Real with Goldie* tonight.

"I'm what?" Merrick yelled.

"If you want to hit someone, hit me. It's my baby your sister is carrying."

Beth had never seen her brother looked so confused. He turned to face her.

"He's the father?"

Beth frowned. This wasn't how she wanted the town to find out.

"Oh my God, just let it go. Yes, he's the father, but I don't need him. I refuse to be with a man who is with me out of guilt."

"Why didn't you tell me?" Merrick sounded wounded.

"I didn't tell anyone."

Gray stepped aside as soon as Merrick let Red go. "She didn't tell me either."

"What the hell, Elizabeth?" Merrick only used her full name when he was upset with her.

"I'm figuring it out. Now leave it alone. You've got your own baby on the way. You don't need to worry about mine." She picked up a bar towel and wiped down the counter. "Obviously Mom said something."

"She told me her condom capers got you too but wouldn't say who the father was except he was a musician. And you were talking to Deanna about getting an intro to Red, so I just assumed."

"Wait," Gray said. "You wanted Deanna to introduce you to Red?"

She shrugged. "That was before I met you." She hated how that sounded all swoony, but it was true. Red didn't stand a chance once she met Gray.

"Not my type anyway," Red said.

Deanna laughed. "True, because you have an IQ over 50."

Merrick pointed at Gray. "You will do right by her."

"I will, but not because you demand it but because I want to."

"Do I get a say so?" Beth asked.

"No," the entire table yelled in unison to her question.

Samantha and Deanna walked over to Beth and hugged her.

"When are you due?" Samantha asked.

Deanna laughed. "June seventh, give or take a day or two if I'm right. If your 'oh shit' comment that day your mom confessed to treachery is an indicator, we got pregnant the same day."

Beth looked at Gray as if to say, I told you so. "It will thrill my mom it's out. Now she can work on the nurseries."

"Your mom is crazy."

Beth laughed. "Certifiable, but she's a wonderful mom." Beth thought about the conversation with her mom about her own missing father. Her mother was probably right to raise her kids on her own. There was no point in making a man do what he didn't want to do.

"Can we talk?"

She looked up at Gray's earnest eyes. "I'm working."

"What about after work?"

She let out a breath, but it came out a growl. "I'll be sleeping."

"Come on, Beth. Give me a chance to make this all right."

"Why? Is it because you feel guilty?" She moved down the bar, gathering the empty beer mugs, and he moved with her, leaning in when he could.

"No, it's because we have stuff to talk about."

She shifted and walked back to the sink where she dropped all the glasses into the waiting sudsy water.

"I've got nothing to say to you." She appreciated he was back and wanted to talk, but she questioned his motives. She couldn't figure out what changed his mind from "I want proof" to "we're having a baby."

"Did I miss anything?" Cannon asked as he

walked out of the hallway.

Beth laughed. "Well, I'm pregnant, and Red got punched in the nose."

Cannon's eyes widened. "You got pregnant while I napped?"

"No, I've been pregnant but haven't said anything. Is that a problem?"

Cannon rubbed his face. "Not as long as you don't bitch at me. I've dealt with enough mood swings to last a lifetime." He looked past her. "Did you say someone punched Red?"

"My brother did."

Cannon pulled a mug of beer and sipped it. "He probably deserved it." He looked between Beth and Red. "Oh my God, is he the father?"

"No," Gray shouted. "I'm the father." He pointed to Beth's tummy. "That's my baby, and she's my girl."

"Okay then," Cannon said. "Take a nap, and the whole world tilts."

Beth wanted to set things straight. "This is his baby, but I'm not his girl."

Gray walked around the bar and kissed her. As soon as his lips touched hers, her entire body ignited. She melted into him, and her brain stopped working while his tongue did delicious things to her mouth. He pulled away and looked down at her. "Are you sure?"

CHAPTER TWENTY-TWO

Women were hard to figure out. Just when he thought he had a clue, they changed things on him. Gray wondered if there was a particular class they gave to girls called "how to mess with a man's mind."

After that kiss last night, he walked out of the bar and went home. He was confident she'd come knocking when she finished her shift, but she didn't, and he fell asleep on the couch waiting for her.

When he woke this morning, she was gone. All day long he'd been glancing out the window, waiting for her to return. He even sent her a text asking if they could talk, but she didn't answer, which worried him. Was she ignoring his message, or was there something wrong?

It was funny how things changed for him once he removed the roadblock to his heart. He found himself feeling things he hadn't allowed himself to experience in years—like hope and longing and happiness.

It was more than just a throbbing in his jeans. It was a vibration that moved through his cells and landed with a thud in his chest.

He paced his living room, waiting for her return until he couldn't stand it any longer. Figuring she went straight to work from wherever she'd been, he walked out his door and headed to Bishop's Brewhouse.

At the bar, Doc was sipping his beer. He looked at Gray and patted the chair beside him. "Come on over, son. You look like you could use an ear." Doc pointed to his. "You know you get two of them and only one mouth because you're supposed to listen twice as much as you speak. The one thing that keeps growing as you age is your ears, which I imagine is God's way of telling us older folks to pay attention."

Gray took a seat next to the wise old man, but his eyes scanned the room, looking for Beth.

"She isn't here."

Trying to play dumb, Gray asked, "Who?"

Doc moved his lips back and forth, making his

bushy mustache dance across his face. "We both know who."

He smiled because playing dumb with Doc never worked in anyone's favor. He was too observant. "She didn't tell me she was going somewhere today."

Doc twirled his mug around, and the light from the bar signs danced off the glass, making his beer look multicolored.

"Does she owe you an explanation? I didn't think you two were a thing."

"She's having my baby, Doc."

"That doesn't make her your woman. That only makes her a mom and you a dad. The other takes commitment and hard work."

"I'm willing to try."

Doc's cheek vibrated with the *pfft* sound that came out of his mouth. "A wise green guy named Yoda once said, 'Do or do not. There is no try.'"

"How do I do that when she won't let me in?" He turned on his stool, looking for Cannon. "And how do I get a beer?"

Doc slipped from the stool and went behind the bar. "It's self-serve until Goldie comes in at six. What'll it be." Doc bent over and took a frosted mug from the freezer and stood behind the taps like he'd been bartending his entire life.

"I'll take a Stella, please." He pulled out his wallet and left a ten on the counter.

"You buying mine too?"

Gray wanted to laugh because Doc suckered him out of a beer every time he sat next to the man, but he had to admit that Doc's counsel was worth far more than what he paid.

"Of course."

Doc leaned over and grabbed his half-empty mug. "Well, in that case, I'll have another. You'll need to put more out there, and don't forget my tip."

Gray's jaw dropped, but he did as Doc told him.

When Doc rounded the bar and took his seat, he turned to Gray and asked, "Do you love her?"

The scruff of his beard scratched his palm as he rubbed his chin in contemplation. "My heart says yes, but my head says I'm crazy." He gulped his beer and let the fizz tickle down. "She's so real, and I'm not used to that. I'm trained to think the worst and expect it. Do you know how many women want what I have?"

"Son, now you listen to me. What you have ain't nothing if you don't get to share it with someone. Let me tell you a story."

Doc cleared his throat, and Gray got comfortable because he knew he wouldn't go anywhere until Doc was finished.

"I've had two great loves in my life. The first was my Phyllis. That girl had me all tied in knots the first time I saw her. Pretty little thing in a dress and saddle shoes. Great legs too, but what I saw first was her heart." Doc sipped his beer and looked straight ahead like he saw a movie.

"When this town was built, we had a schoolhouse over near where the Dawson Ranch is. The old building still stands. I own that piece of property because some of my fondest memories came from that school."

"Go on." Gray loved to imagine Doc as a small boy.

"Folks around here weren't wealthy. My Phyllis came from a family of hard workers, but they didn't have much. I gave her my prize hog so her family could eat."

"Were you trying to butter up her father?"

Doc chuckled. "Son, I was just trying not to meet the end of his shotgun."

"Sounds like a wise move."

"It was more than that, though. I knew they struggled to make ends meet, and by helping out, I was proving that I could step up and take responsibility. Keep in mind that my family had more than enough. And if there's one thing I've learned, it's that you never need more than enough."

"How does this apply to me?"

Doc tapped him on the head. "Think, son, if you could only choose one thing, would it be money or Beth?"

"Ahh, you're asking me if Beth would be enough."

Doc sipped his beer and stayed silent.

Gray closed his eyes and imagined a world without money. He'd lived in that world and survived. His family always had enough, but not much more, and they were happy. He'd also lived without Beth and survived, but if he had to choose one to live without, it would be money. It's nice to have and makes life so much easier, but it doesn't make you laugh, warm your bed, fill your heart, or have your baby.

"You started about the two loves in your life. What drew you to them?"

Doc turned to face him. "Integrity and heart. Remember that old schoolhouse and the poor people of Aspen Cove? One day we were getting our lunches out of our bags, and a little boy named Tyler forgot to bring his. That's what he said anyway, but we all knew he didn't have one because he often only had a slice of bread. I watched Phyllis open her lunch and look at it. I sat next to her, so I heard her stomach growl, but she took out her sandwich and the apple her mother had sliced into sections and gave it to that boy. If I hadn't already been in love with that girl, I was that day because she didn't give from her excess. She gave from her need. She was willing to do without just so a little boy didn't have to."

"Did you give her your lunch?"

"I tried, but in the end, we shared, and that was another lesson I learned. The feeling you get from sharing fills you up." Doc finished his beer and slid the cup across the bar. "So, let me ask the questions again? Do you love her?"

"Yes."

"When did you know?"

He thought back to the night she tried to make a fire. "It was the night she cried over a dead fish."

Doc slid from his stool. "There you have it."

"You said you had two loves in your life. What about Agatha?"

Doc laughed. "You got those women who are like spun sugar, and they make everything sweeter. That was Phyllis. And then you got those who test your wits and try your patience, but it's their tenacity that keeps you coming back. Agatha loves me, and she tells me I can't do any better than her, and you know what, she's right."

"Thanks, Doc. I think I maybe owe you another beer."

"Nope, I think we're good." He lifted his brow. "You good? All clear in the head about this woman?"

"Yes, now my job is to make her all clear in the head about me."

"Wherever she is, she'll be back by the end of the week."

"How do you know?"

Doc shook his head. "Can't say." He walked to the door. "If you need anything, Cannon is sleeping in the back. The poor man gets his best sleep at work. I have to give him credit. He's figuring out how to make sure he's all in with Sage and the baby. If he gets a little rest here, he can take all the night stuff. Remember, a happy wife equals a happy life."

The door closed behind Doc, and Gray smiled as he sat in the silent, empty bar. He was going to make Beth happy, even if it killed him trying to make that happen.

CHAPTER TWENTY-THREE

She still couldn't believe the for sale sign in her mother's front yard.

"Are you sure you want to move to Aspen Cove?" Beth said, "I mean ... there isn't even a library."

"I know, but there's a bookstore, and the last time I was there, that sweet thing Natalie said she'd love to hire someone because she wants to focus on starting a family. I've got enough years in the system to retire. Besides, what's here in Aurora if both of my kids are in Aspen Cove? And now I'm getting two grandbabies." Her mother blushed. "Then there's that sweet cowboy who took me for a cup of coffee in Copper Creek on Thanksgiving night. He's a nice man."

"I can't believe you have a date. I've been there for so much longer, and I've got nothing." Beth plopped onto the couch in her mother's living room. "Why is my life such a mess?" She drove to her mom's yesterday because she needed advice. She could have called, but after that kiss, Gray wasn't staying away, and at this point, she was sure she wanted him to. The problem was, she didn't know his motives or what caused the total about-face.

"Honey, we talked about this last night. If Merrick's father had taken a moment to truly think about what he was losing and came back to me, I would have let him back in my life. The man vanished like fog on a sunny day. And if your father hadn't been all kinds of wrong, I would have gladly let him be a part of our lives, but some men aren't made for commitment."

"How do I know if Gray is?"

Her mom took a seat in the leather chair next to the wall of bookshelves.

"Seems to me like you guys have a communication problem. You've got your doctor's appointment soon. Maybe you should invite him. There's nothing like a baby's heartbeat to make them stay or run. It's an either/or type of situation."

"You're telling me to test him?"

"Oh, honey, when women test men, we are ultimately setting them up to fail. I wouldn't call it a test. Invite him, and if he wants to come, you know he's interested in being part of the baby's life. If he doesn't, then you know you're on your own." Her mother pulled Beth's baby picture from a nearby shelf. "You were the sweetest thing. I'm not going to say it was easy, but I had to make a choice when I found out I was pregnant. Your father was well-off, which could have benefited me, but it would have worked in his favor too. He could have fought me at every turn, and what was the point ... money? You have options. Gray is a man of means, so you have a right to ask for support, but that choice is yours. All I have to say is weigh your options. How much in-terference and influence do you want the man to have? The more he's involved, the higher the stakes."

"I get that." She hung her head. Deep inside, she was so proud of her mom for the job she did raising Merrick and her. "I just wish I'd had some contact with my father, even if he was a certifiable asshole. I wish I had been able to meet him and know for myself. Why the big secret? Who was he?"

Her mother laughed. "You want to know?"

Beth nodded. "I think I need to know."

"Okay, but just don't get star struck. People like him might wear Tom Ford suits, but he still wipes his ass with toilet paper."

Leave it to her mom to equalize.

"My dad is famous?"

Elsa shook her head and smiled. "He's not Tom Cruise."

"Tell me."

"Your father is Senator Parker Noland." Beth sat there and stared at her like she was speaking in tongues. Her father was a politician—one who preached family values. "What a hypocrite." Beth had seen things about him from time to time in the news. He had a beautiful wife and two daughters. He went to church every weekend, kissed babies on the campaign trail, and slept with her mom. "How did you meet him?"

"At the library."

"And you didn't know he was a senator?"

Her mother squirmed in her seat. It was kind of fun for Beth to watch her mom on the other side of the interrogation.

"He wasn't a senator when I met him. He was a young lawyer."

"Did you know he was married with kids?"

"Of course not. I would never get involved with a man who had a wife. I'm a lot of things, but not a home-wrecker. He would come over to my place since I had your brother. He was always good to Merrick. I suppose your brother was the son Parker never had."

"What an asshole."

Her mother lifted her shoulders. "He had good qualities too, but honesty wasn't one of them."

"What do you think he'd do if I tried to contact him?"

"I have no idea, but it is your right. My only warning would be not to expect much from him."

"I have very low expectations for most men."

Her mother frowned. "I'm sorry about that. My experiences shouldn't jade you. Most men who love you want to please you, and they will rise to the height of the bar you set. Don't set the bar too low. Let Gray reach for your love. He'll want it, and you'll be happier if you are honest from the start. Now get back home and see if he's worth your efforts."

"I will." They rose and met in the middle for a hug. "I love you, Mom."

"Love you too, honey."

Her mother walked her to the door, and Beth called the dogs, who came running from the kitchen. Since she only spent the night, the rest of the menagerie stayed at home with extra food.

Once she got everyone in the car, she backed out but didn't get far because Senator Noland's name kept pinging around in her head.

She pulled over and looked up his office number at the capitol building in Colorado and dialed. The worst-case scenario would be that he wasn't in town. The best would be that he'd have time to meet her for a coffee.

"Senator Noland's office, this is Marjorie. Can I help you?"

"Yes, hello." Beth's heart shook inside her chest. "This is Elizabeth Buchanan, and I'd like to speak to the Senator, please."

"Is he expecting your call?"

Her stomach tightened, and she was sure she'd lose the oatmeal her mother had fed her.

"No, but please tell him that Elsa Buchanan's daughter is on the line."

"Please hold."

Beth sat on the roadside and waited for what seemed like a lifetime but was only a minute.

The phone clicked, and a deep voice said hello.

"Umm, hi. Do you know who I am?"

He cleared his throat. "Yes, I do. What can I do for you? It's been over thirty years. What do you want?"

Those words were like a slap to the face. "Nothing."

"Why did you call?"

"Because I wanted to know if something deep inside you ever wondered about me."

The lull in conversation was painful. Each second that passed without a response was like a hand twisting her gut. It would be so lovely to hear that he was on the sideline watching her play soccer, or that he came to her first-grade play when she got the part of Mrs. Claus.

"What happened with your mom and me was over long before you were born. I thought we settled it."

She swallowed the lump in her throat. "Settled between you two, but what about me? I had questions all along."

"Listen, I don't know what your mom told you, but I have a family. I wasn't looking for another."

Heat built up inside, and Beth was certain she'd combust. "She told me nothing until I finally asked for the truth. You see, my mom was enough. She never talked bad about you except to say you had lots of good qualities, but honesty wasn't one. I just wanted to know how you could have a child and not even care enough to want to meet her. You are half of who I am."

He took a breath and let it out. "It's just DNA. It's kind of like going to lunch with a person, and you order different things. Your mom was looking for a cheeseburger, and all I had was a glass of water to offer."

"Yeah, well, my mom's a vegetarian now, and she never drinks water." Beth's voice rose until it hurt her ears. "I always hoped there was something

I could learn from you, and I just did. You're an asshole, and I'll never vote for you again."

"You voted for me?" His voice changed to a politician at a rally. "Thanks for your support."

"That was before I got educated." She put her car in gear and pulled away from the curb. "And just so you know, you're going to be a grandfather." She slammed her hand on the steering wheel. "No, scratch that, you would have had to be a father first."

"Elizabeth, I hope that this conversation—"

"Don't worry, your secret is safe with me. I wouldn't want anyone to know I'm related to you. As far as I'm concerned, I was a heavenly conception." She hung up the phone and headed back to Aspen Cove.

All the way back, she thought about Gray. Would he be like her father? Or would he be a better man? She'd give him a chance, but one was all he got. She was prepared to raise their baby on her own. But that thought made her giggle because she lived in Aspen Cove, and there, no one was ever alone.

CHAPTER TWENTY-FOUR

Gray sat near the window like a Labrador waiting for his owner to return. The longer Beth was gone, the more uncomfortable he got. Not with the idea of loving her and being with one person, but with the fact that she was gone, and he didn't know if she was all right. He left her a text telling her he was thinking about her an hour ago, but she didn't respond. Then again, if she had, he would have worried that she was texting and driving. There was more at stake here than ever before. It wasn't only about the baby—it was everything. He'd messed up. He'd let his past influence his future.

While that was common practice for most humans, it wasn't wise. Allison ruined a lot for him. She stole his ability to trust; she took away the dream of having a family, and she made him a bitter man.

He shook his head at the silliness of those thoughts. Allison didn't do those things to him. He allowed it to happen because he was happy to blame someone else for his failings. But this time, it would be different. This time he'd be more self-aware and less self-centered.

The smell of fresh garlic floated through the air. When the pizza was done, his stomach growled. He rolled to his feet, but the glint of the fading sun flashed off the windshield of Beth's SUV as she pulled into her driveway.

He knew he needed to get the pizza out of the oven but feared taking his eyes off her. If he turned his back, she might disappear, so he rushed to the front door.

"Beth," he called, grabbing her attention. "I've got a pizza just coming out of the oven. Come over and have some."

She gave him a weak smile. "I need to feed the animals. Kitty needs a snuggle since I've been gone."

I need a snuggle. "Grab her and their food and come over." He hated to beg but was happy to if he got his way. "Please. It's a combination with double pepperoni, just the way you like it."

He knew he had her when she licked her lips.

When Beth stayed with him, that was a staple in the house. He realized now that it was probably a pregnancy craving, but if it got her to his house, he'd use whatever tactics he had at his disposal.

She stalled for a moment as if contemplating his invite but the smile on her face told him he'd won.

"I'll be over in a few minutes. Do you have extra parmesan?"

"I do."

"What about pepperoncini?"

"I bought a new jar."

"You're the best." She opened the back door to let the dogs out. "Let me get them settled."

"They can come. Just get the cat." He whistled, getting the attention of Gums, who ran toward him. Ozzy followed, with his hind end wagging so hard he fell over twice. "Hello, boys." He missed the mutts and stepped aside while they rushed in, heading straight for the fireplace where Gums curled up first, followed by Ozzy, who nuzzled up to Gums's belly.

Gray pulled the pizza from the oven and waited. He stood at the doorjamb near the kitchen and looked at the pups, all cozy and comfortable. This was near perfect. The only thing missing was Beth and Kitty and Trip and Stevie ... and their baby.

His mind whirled. There was so much to do

and so little time. By his calculations, Beth was going on four months now, which meant he only had five to make her fall madly in love with him. Could it be done?

There was so much to consider. What would happen when he went on tour? Would she come? What if The Resistance offered him the job? Would she be willing to move to Los Angeles so he could record? Was it possible to have it all?

A light tap at the door drew him out of his thoughts. He walked over and opened it. God, she was breathtaking Her cheeks glowed like she'd just swiped on blush, but he could see that her face didn't have any makeup. That was one thing he loved about her. She didn't try to impress him. There wasn't anything phony about her.

He reached out wrapped his arms around her, tugging her in for a hug. "I missed you."

"Wow," she said into his chest. "What's gotten into you?"

"Common sense."

She broke from his embrace and stepped back, looking at him with skepticism. "Still trying to re-cover from the whiplash. Excuse me if you think I'm rude, but one day you're basically accusing me of being a gold digger, and now you're telling me you missed me?"

"Come all the way in, and let's get you fed. You must be hungry."

"Do I look hungry?"

He chuckled. "Yes, you do. Besides, when I was hugging, I heard your tummy growl." He looked down and realized she didn't have Kitty. "Where's the cat?"

"She was happily sleeping on the sofa, and I didn't want to bother her." She lifted her bag. "I brought the boys' food with me. Can I borrow two bowls?"

Gray wrapped his arm around her shoulders and led her into the kitchen. "Hand me the food, and I'll take care of it." He held out his hand and waited for her to give him the baggies of food—one grain-free for Ozzy, the other needing a good soak in warm water for Gums. "You want some tea?"

She took a seat at the table. "I'd love some. Can I help with anything?"

He shook his head. "Nope, I got it. You just rest."

He pulled out two bowls and prepared the dogs' food like she'd shown him before.

"Where did you disappear to?" He whistled for the dogs before putting the bowls in opposite corners of the kitchen. They immediately appeared and went straight to eating.

"I went to see my mom."

"Oh. That's good." The cupboard door creaked when he opened it and took out two plates. "One or two slices to start?"

"Two," she said.

He got the pepperoncini and parmesan from the refrigerator and sat across from her. "How are you feeling?"

She stared at him. "I'm good." She cocked her head from side to side. "Just glad the morning sickness is over. That was brutal."

"Did you have it when you were here?"

She frowned. "Maybe once or twice."

His shoulders sagged. "I didn't know. I wish I had. I would have ..."

She set her slice down and looked at him. "Would have what? Accused me of having motives earlier? I'm glad you didn't know, or I might have been staying in my car."

"I would have never kicked you out. That's not the man I am."

She rearranged the peppers on her pizza. "What kind of man are you, Gray?"

He took a bite and considered the next words he'd say. "I'm the man who loves deeply but trusts cautiously. Honestly, I'm an idiot. I let a woman who has no moral base define how I saw the world, and that was wrong of me."

"Not all women are after your money. Take me, for instance, I want nothing from you."

That sliced straight to his core.

"I'd give you everything you need."

She swallowed hard, and a tear pooled in the corner of her eye. "That's the thing. Anything I'd ask of you would never be for me." Her hand fell to her stomach. "And I don't want you to step up for the baby unless you want to be there."

He reached across the table to take her hand. "But I do."

"Since when? I can still hear the words you said to me in the parking lot."

"That wasn't what I meant."

"But it's what you said."

He inhaled and let it go. "That was the asshole part. I've had time to think, and I'm sorry." He squeezed her hand. "I too have a mother, and I called her when I was in Denver. I told her everything, and I swear, if she could reach through the phone, she would have slapped me upside the head."

The tear slipped from Beth's eye, but a giggle escaped her lips. "I would have liked to see that."

"I bet." He picked the olives off his pizza.

"Why do you order it with olives when you don't like them?"

"Because you like them."

She narrowed her eyes. "You ordered this pizza knowing I'd eat some?"

"No, I ordered this pizza, hoping you would. I have a lot to answer for. Let me apologize again. I was an idiot."

She swiped at the tear with her free hand. He was grateful she hadn't pulled the hand he held back.

"Yes, you were."

He chuckled. How this woman tied him in knots so fast was a mystery.

"Glad we agree on something."

"It's a start."

"A start to what?"

"To hopefully being friends."

He scooted his chair toward hers and placed his elbows on his knees, leaning forward to get closer to her.

"We are more than friends." He held up his hands. "Can I touch my child?"

Her jaw dropped. "You sure you don't want a DNA test?"

He winced. "I'm sorry." He leaned forward and rested his head in her lap. "I know the baby is mine." He lifted himself and tapped his chest. "I feel it right here."

She grabbed his hand mid-air and pulled it toward her stomach. "I feel little ripples from time to time, but I'm not sure if it's the baby or what I ate. All you'll feel is my fat."

"Nope." He splayed his fingers across her middle. "What I feel is your love for someone you've never met. You're a good woman, and deep inside, I knew that, but I let an old record play on repeat. You said you want to be friends, but what if I want more?"

She set her hand on top of his. "I don't think you know what you want. This is all new to both of us. Particularly you because I've had four months to get used to the idea."

He looked at the ceiling and then back at her eyes. They were as green as clover. "I want this. I want you." He gathered her hands in his and brought them to his lips. "Before I even knew about the baby, I was trying to figure out how I could keep you. I even considered ruining your furnace just to get you back here. My life is empty without you." He kissed her knuckles.

She pulled her hands away and laid them on her lap. "Here's the thing. I can't have you in my life if you're going to waffle. You're in or out." A look of sadness crossed her face. "I had my first conversation with my father today on the way back from my mother's. I never knew him. My mother used to tell me I was a heavenly conception. She was protecting me. My father, he's... he's a public figure. I always wished I'd had some kind of contact with him, but now I get why I didn't. He's an asshole. He wanted nothing to do with me. I was just the product of a sperm that swam astray."

"Oh, honey. I'm sorry." He went to reach for her, but she pulled back.

"No, don't be. My mom did what was best for me, and I have to do what's best for my child."

"Our child."

"That's the thing, Gray. I don't want you around if you'll be bitter about it. I don't want you taking out your displeasure on our baby. I just want to have a happy child who is loved by both of us, and if that's not possible, then I'll love him or her enough to compensate. You're in, or you're out. It's not fair to the baby if you can't decide."

"I get it. I'm—"

"Think about it before you commit. And no matter what you choose, it's okay because we all have limits."

"Beth ..." What could he say? She was very pedantic about everything, and he had to respect her for that.

She took her last bite of pizza and pushed her plate away. "I have an appointment tomorrow morning with Doc Parker. I'm having an ultrasound, and I'd like you to come if you want to, but I'll understand if you don't."

He pulled her to him and wrapped his arms around her. "Beth, I'm going to be there. Just like you're not Allison, I'm not your father. I want to be a part of our baby's life. I'll earn your trust."

She leaned back and smiled. "I think you just might surprise me."

"Can I kiss my baby mama?"

"Should we make this more complicated?"

He brushed his lips across hers. "Absolutely."

CHAPTER TWENTY-FIVE

It was so hard to leave him last night after that kiss, but she had to. Life was complicated enough, and adding attraction on top of other hormones at work was a bad idea. Until she knew what Gray truly wanted from her, she couldn't expose her heart. Right now, everything was muddled, and giving him her body felt like giving him her heart.

She finished dressing and fed the dogs. In about fifteen minutes, she'd know how serious he was about being a part of her life. If he was at Doc's, then at least he was ready to dip his toe in the deep end, but if he wasn't, she would know he wasn't diving in at all.

"You three be good," she said to her babies. She gave Trip's cage a little rattle and looked in on

Stevie Wonder, who happily swam in circles. "Wish me luck."

She knew she was late going to her first prenatal appointment, but fear drove her response. Now she was no longer fearful but excited. When she looked at things with clarity, it wasn't so hard to accept. Yes, she was a single mother, but she wasn't alone.

She picked up her purse and walked out the door, only to find Gray leaning against his car. In his hand was a steaming cup of tea.

"I'll drive." He opened the passenger door and stepped aside.

For a moment, she was stunned into paralysis. Deep inside, she knew he'd come because Gray was a good man. She still couldn't erase what he told her from her memory. *I even considered ruining your furnace just to get you back here. My life is empty without you.* It repeatedly played in her mind, making her feel giddy.

Her brain finally connected to her feet, and she moved toward him.

"We could have met at Doc's office."

"Why would we do that when I'm right here?"

She considered what her mother said about him possibly running once he heard the heartbeat.

"What if you freak out and need space?"

He crowded her close to the open door. "Baby, I don't need space. I need you." He held out the tea.

"Here's your fave. I thought we could grab lunch after the appointment and then maybe go shopping for some baby things. Let's make it a day."

Her breath hitched. "You're giving me whiplash again."

"I'm not going anywhere. I'm here for you and" —he placed his palm on her belly—"our baby. No matter what happens, I'll be here for you both."

She hated to be a cynic, but she had to trust her mother, and she'd withhold all hopes and dreams until she looked into his eyes once he heard their baby.

"I'm excited. What about you?"

He helped her inside and kissed her gently. "In truth, I'm scared shitless, but I'm also excited."

She smiled against his soft lips that disappeared too soon. He helped buckle her in like he was taking care of precious cargo.

"I get it. I'm scared too." And she was, for many reasons. Her body would change. Her life would be fuller but more complicated. She'd have to juggle motherhood and a job. There were bills to be paid. It was all so complicated, and yet, it would happen regardless. Life was going to progress whether she was afraid or not. The baby would be born whether or not Beth was ready.

He rounded the car and climbed into the driver's seat.

"We can be scared together." He squeezed her hand before he put the car into reverse and backed out of the driveway.

As they drove down the street, Beth glanced at the houses in the empty neighborhood and wondered how many would be filled with new families next year. Aspen Cove was growing, and while it would never be as big as one of Denver's suburbs, it would still grow to capacity over time. Children would play kickball in the streets, and the park would be packed with families on the weekends. Someday, they wouldn't be able to hold the Thanksgiving feast in The Guild Creative Center because there would be too many people. The thought of belonging to such a community made her smile because she hardly knew her neighbors in Aurora. Everyone was so busy making a life that they forgot to have one.

"You ready, love?"

Calling her love sent a tingle racing through her veins. Could it be this easy? Could falling in love with Gray be any more perfect?

"Yes, I'm ready."

He got out of the car and raced to her side to help her out. When she stood on the curb in front of Doc's, he held her hand and walked her inside.

Agatha stood behind the register. "I'll tell them you're here."

"Them?" Gray asked.

Beth looked up at him. "Yes, Dr. Lydia will be there too. Since Sage is on maternity leave, her sister is doubling as a nurse." She laughed. "Or maybe Doc is Lydia's nurse since she's my primary care physician."

"I'm no nurse," Doc said as he appeared from behind a Pepto Bismol display. "Let's go, you two, and meet your baby."

Gray was a step ahead of her the entire way down the hallway. He wasn't running away—yet.

Doc took a dressing gown from the cupboard and set it on the table. "Undress from the waist down. Lydia and I will be back in a minute." Doc walked out.

Gray looked at the door and then back at her. "You want me to leave while you change?"

She didn't know what made her laugh, but she did. "It's not like you haven't seen it."

He nodded and smiled. "True, but I want you to be comfortable."

She took off her jacket and laid it on the chair, then unbuttoned and unzipped her pants. She shimmied them down until she got to her shoes, and she removed them all at once. Gray took the pants from her and folded them, setting them on the chair with her coat, but his eyes never left her center, and she wasn't sure if he was looking at the sexy red panties that she wore just in case he joined her or the tiny mound that was their baby.

"Wow, you look amazing."

She thumbed the sides of her panties and slid them down her thighs. "You like them?"

"Yes, I like them, but it's more than that. You're beautiful. I'm sure you'd be hot in anything."

She rubbed her hand over her belly. "Look at this now because it's only getting bigger."

He smiled. "Can't wait. There's nothing more beautiful than a woman carrying a child. Nothing sexier than you carrying mine."

She shook her head. "What did your mother say to you to make you change your mind?"

He grimaced as if her words wounded him. "She talked to me about my father. She told me what I already knew about myself: I'm a runner but not a quitter. I may have run from you, but I would never quit you. She also reminded me that trust was earned, and you had earned mine, but I needed to earn yours."

She tugged on the hospital gown and sat on the table.

"Do you think your mother would like me?"

"My mother will love you."

A knock sounded at the door, and Lydia peeked her head inside. "You ready?"

"Yes." Beth squirmed on the exam table. "We're

listening to the heartbeat, right?" The closer she got to hearing her baby, the more excited she became.

"We're not only going to listen to your little peanut, but we're also going to see the little one." She turned to look at Doc, who was wheeling out a machine from the closet.

"We're doing an ultrasound?" She was three parts excited and one part fearful. The afraid part was because she hadn't budgeted for an ultrasound. She didn't know what one cost. "Umm, how much is that?"

"Doesn't matter," Gray said. "We're going to meet our baby."

"But—"

A kiss shut down her arguments. When Gray pulled back, he looked at her with such affection. "No buts. You'll have whatever you want."

She shook her head. "I only want what I need. Is an ultrasound something I need?"

Doc rolled it over to the edge of the exam table. "I think your beau needs it."

"He's not—"

"Oh, yes, I am. Now, let's get this started. Where do you want me?"

Doc moved to her right and pointed to the other side of the table. You stand there and watch this screen.

Lydia covered her lower half with a sheet and

exposed only her stomach. "This is going to be a little cold. We warm it, but it never seems warm enough." She squeezed a blob of gel onto Beth's tummy while Doc powered up the machine. He dipped the wand into the gel and moved it around while she and Gray stared at the screen like they were waiting for a new release. And they kind of were. This was a new production, and they were experiencing its debut.

Her womb's shape emerged on the screen, and inside it was what Lydia called their peanut. Doc messed with a dial, and the room filled with a whooshing sound.

"That is your baby's heartbeat," Lydia said. "Sounds very healthy." She moved to the screen and pointed out the head and body and the little arms and legs.

Beth looked at Gray and saw the tears in his eyes. He was overwrought with emotion, as was she. Moving on that screen was their future.

A ringing filled the air that drowned out the sound of the heartbeat. Beth looked at Gray, who fumbled in his pocket for his phone.

"I'm sorry." He looked at the screen, and his eyes grew big.

"Do you need to take that?" she asked.

Gray shoved the phone back inside his pocket. "Nope. You're more important."

The baby's heartbeat filled the air again, and again his phone rang.

"Son, just answer it," Doc said. "They want to talk to you."

Gray looked down at Beth. "Honey, do you mind?"

She smiled. How could she? This man beside her looked at her with so much love.

"No, take it."

It got to the fourth ring before he answered with a curt, "This is Gray."

Beth watched as his expression changed from surprised, to troubled, to content.

"Hold on a second." He looked at her. "Hey, love. This is Bryson from The Resistance. They've offered me the job as lead guitarist for the band."

A lump came from deep inside her and lodged in her throat. He didn't have to run. His job would take him away. How was she supposed to respond? She knew this was the one opportunity he had been waiting for. How could she not be happy for him? The problem was, she was devastated for herself.

She swallowed her pride and her disappointment and put on the best smile she could muster. "That's wonderful. It's what you always wanted." She swallowed several times, hoping not to gag on the sorrow.

He took his phone off mute, and while everyone

was there to listen, he said, "You know what, Bryson? I just looked into my girlfriend's eyes and saw how hurt she'd be if I left her. In truth, I don't want to leave her. I'm going to be a father, and while joining your band has always been a goal of mine, having a family has been my dream. I think I'm going to pass on the gig. Everything I need is right here in Aspen Cove."

Beth didn't hear him say goodbye, but she heard Doc tell him he was proud of his choice.

"You want a picture of your baby?" Lydia asked.

The tears ran down her cheeks while she nodded.

"Can we have two?" Gray asked. "I have to show off my kid."

Lydia clicked a button and printed the photos. "Next time, we can accurately tell the sex of the baby if you want to know."

Beth lifted to look at the screen. "You'll be able to tell?"

"Yep, but you and daddy should talk it over. My sister didn't want to know. She said there are very few surprises in life and the sex of her child was one of them."

"How is little Michael?" Gray asked.

Lydia laughed. "He's ruling their world, but that's what babies do. They change your life."

"I'm counting on it," Gray said.

Lydia wiped off Beth's stomach while Doc cleaned the machine and wheeled it toward the storage room.

"Here's your baby, mom and dad." Lydia looked at Gray. "Up to you and Beth, but I'm going to do an exam, and then she'll be ready to go."

"You want me to stay or go?" Gray asked.

Beth could see in his eyes that he was both happy to stay but somewhat apprehensive.

"How about you get us a booth at the diner? I'm starving."

"Deal." He was out of the room faster than she could blink, but she knew he wasn't running.

As soon as the door closed, Lydia started her exam.

"I feel that something big just went down. Am I right?"

Beth could hardly contain the emotion. She nodded. "He just gave up everything for the baby."

Lydia chuckled. "Oh, honey, you didn't see the way he looked at you. That wasn't about that baby; he gave it up for you. The baby is just a bonus. That man loves you."

Deep inside, Beth knew that to be the truth. She felt it in every cell of her being.

Lydia finished her exam and gave Beth all the details, including her due date, which was the same day as Deanna. Go figure. After she left,

Beth got dressed and went to the front of the office to pay.

Agatha smiled. "Your man took care of everything."

"My man," she repeated. "I like the sound of that."

She left the doctor feeling renewed, like her life had a complete plot twist for the better.

When she entered the diner, she found Gray showing off his baby picture to anyone who would look, and a feeling of pride enveloped her.

He saw her, and his entire face lit up. That was what Gray looked like completely happy, and she always wanted to see him like that.

"Come and sit," he said excitedly. "Tell me what you want."

Rather than sit across from him, she scooted into the booth next to him. "You, Gray. I want you."

"Oh, baby, you have me. You had me that first night when you climbed on—."

"Gray," she squealed with embarrassment.

"I was going to say, I fell in love with you that first night when you *climbed on* the stage and completely slaughtered Frampton's 'Baby, I love your way.'"

"You love me?" Her heart danced in her chest.

"How could I not? You're gorgeous and giving and you rescue animals. You even rescued me."

She leaned into him and laid her head on his arm. "I did?"

"Yes. I was falling, and you caught me."

"Can I confess something to you?"

"That you love me?"

She frowned. "How did you know?"

"I see it in your eyes. It's the same look you get when I bring you cake, but sexier."

She laughed. "You're impossible."

"Yep, but you're possible, and you're not a quitter, so I imagine my heart is safe in your hands."

She lifted to kiss him. "I love you, Gray Stratton."

"Love you too, Liz." He winked and kissed her more deeply.

"What's it going to be, lovebirds?" Maisey asked.

"Blue-plate special, of course," Beth said.

"But you don't even know what it is," Maisey answered.

Beth sat taller and looked straight at Gray. "Sometimes you just have to take a chance. The risk could be worth the reward."

Maisey walked away, and Gray pulled out his phone.

"Who are you calling?"

"My mom, I want her to talk to her future daughter-in-law."

CHAPTER TWENTY-SIX

FOUR WEEKS LATER

"Do you like the green and yellow or the orange and yellow?" Elsa asked Gray.

He smiled and looked at Beth, who was tugging at a too-small T-shirt she wouldn't wear after today.

"Should we tell her?"

Elsa eyed her daughter, then stared at Gray. She had a look that would scare the pants off lesser men, but Gray grew up with a mother just like her. Elsa Buchanan was a storm that you either avoided or marveled at. Since she had brought Beth into this world by herself, Gray opted for the latter.

"I suppose we should before she gets her heart set on a color scheme." Beth went over to her mother's paint chips and pulled out two. "We're going with blue and lime green."

Elsa furrowed her brows. "Honey, blue is ..." she cocked her head and smiled. "Oh my God, does that mean we're having a boy?"

Gray moved to where Beth stood next to her mom and placed his hands on Beth's tummy. "We found out just this morning before you drove up." Gray whipped out his wallet and produced the newest ultrasound picture, which clearly showed he had a son.

"Meet your grandson."

Elsa took the picture, and her eyes misted over. Gray knew the feeling all too well. There was something about knowing you were part of the reason a new human was coming into this world that made him weep.

"A grandson ..." She looked at the paint chips. "I think the color scheme will be perfect. In fact, could anything get more perfect?"

Gray knew this was his moment. "It could."

Both women turned to face him.

"What's more perfect than blue and lime green?" Beth asked with a pout. "I thought you loved it."

"I do, and I love you. The only thing that can make this more perfect is for you to say yes."

She stared at him. "To what?"

He dropped to a knee in front of her and freed the ring he'd put in his pocket that morning.

"Say yes to me, Beth. Say yes to us. Will you be the mother of my son and the keeper of my heart?" He opened the box to the ring he'd chosen for her. Beth wasn't big diamonds and bling. She was sentimental, so he got her a band of intertwined yellow gold and platinum representing the two of them woven together without an end.

"You want to marry me?"

"I'm asking to do just that."

Beth looked at the ring and smiled, but she didn't reach for it. "I don't want to get married just because I'm pregnant."

Elsa laughed. "I wish I had a man on his knee who wanted to spend the rest of his life with me."

He shifted, still holding the ring and staring into Beth's eyes. "You know, if the whole pregnancy were a hoax, I'd still want to marry you. How could I not love a woman who takes in strays and loves the most damaged souls until they are whole again? You made me whole again." He took the ring from the box and held it to her finger. "What do you say?"

She let him slip the ring on. "I say, I'll consider it if you take me to the store for a bag of Fritos."

He chuckled. If Beth had one craving, it was Fritos. That kid was his. "It's a deal. You wear my ring while you're thinking about it. And if you say yes, I'll keep you in Fritos for the rest of your life."

"Is that a promise?"

"Yes."

She tugged his hand until he stood. "Then, yes."

"Yes?" He picked her up and spun her in circles.

"Yes, but put me down."

"I'm never letting you go."

"You'll have to because I want that first install-ment of Fritos."

"While you two practice Frito foreplay, I'm heading into Copper Creek to get paint. I'm also supposed to meet that Mason Van der whatever to see a house on Hyacinth."

"Mom," Beth said. "If I'm marrying Gray, we won't need two houses. What if you move into mine and take over the payments?"

She looked at the chips. "That's an excellent idea, but lime green and blue will never do for me. And what about a carpenter? Is there a good one in town? You know how much I love my books and that means shelves, lots of shelves." She turned around in a circle. "I have so much to do."

"Baxter or Wes can help you with that."

Gray bent over and kissed Elsa on the cheek. "Do you need anything from the store?"

"A man willing to bend a knee and give me a ring. Do they carry those at the corner store?"

"I'll see what I can find." He slung his arm over Beth's shoulders. "You ready future, Mrs. Stratton."

"Ready, Mr. Stratton."

———

They entered the store to find Jewel high on a ladder, dismantling some shelving.

"Be careful up there. I'd hate to see you fall," Gray said.

"Oh, I've already fallen as low as I can go." She gave him a charming smile and went back to ripping out the shelving from the wall. "I've got two bags of Fritos left."

"How did you know?" Beth asked.

"I've learned to pay attention. It was never a strong suit before, but I'm getting better at it."

"Always good to pay attention," Gray added. "What are you doing?"

"I'm starting from scratch."

He got the idea that she was talking about more than the store. He'd met Jewel a few times. She was always nice but seemed cautious. He often found her behind the counter making lists.

The door opened, and in walked a man in a suit. No one in Aspen Cove dressed up like they were heading for the boardroom.

Beth grabbed the two bags of Fritos corn chips

and tugged on Gray's belt loop. "Talk about perfect timing. That's Mason Van der Veen."

He moved into the store and looked around.

"Hey, Mason," Beth said. "I know you're here to meet with my mom, but I think she's going to cancel."

"What? Why didn't she call me?"

"Everything just happened today." Beth held up her hand and pointed to the ring. "He asked me to marry him, and I said yes. We don't need two houses, so Mom is going to move into mine."

"Did you say your mom was looking at a house? Where?"

Mason looked at Jewel as if he just realized there was a woman on a ladder the entire time.

"Hyacinth." Mason's eyes grew enormous. "Hey, I know you, you're J—"

The shelf came tumbling down, whacking Mason on the top of the head. He crashed to a heap on the linoleum floor.

"Oh, damn," Jewel said. "Maybe I haven't hit rock bottom yet."

"Shall we get Doc?" Beth asked.

Mason stirred and held his hand in the air. "Nope, I'm good."

"Are you sure?" Gray asked.

"Yep." He looked at Jewel and gave his head a

shake. "I think I have a house to sell the lady." He smiled at her. "What should I call you?"

"Jewel. I'm Jewel."

"Right," Mason said with a skeptical tone.

Gray watched the odd exchange but let it go. "Can I pay for these?" He pointed to the bags of chips. "It's part of the dowry I promised my future wife."

Jewel waved them off. "Consider it an engagement gift." She climbed down the ladder and helped Mason to his feet before turning to Gray and Beth. With a smile that didn't reach her eyes, she said, "Have a great day."

Gray stared at the odd couple for the briefest of moments before he escorted his fiancée out the door.

"Were we just dismissed?" Beth asked.

"Summarily." Gray pulled his phone from his pocket and looked at the screen. "How long do you think your mother will be gone?"

"What did you have in mind?" Beth whispered in that sultry way that made his entire body react.

He helped her into the car and made his way around to the driver's side.

"I thought I'd take my fiancée home and show her how much I love her."

"Ooh," she cooed. "Tell you what, if Mom's there, we'll go directly to your place."

"Our place, love. What's mine is yours."

She turned to face him. "Speaking of yours, do you want me to sign a prenup? I mean, I bring nothing to our union."

"You bring everything." He sucked a breath between his teeth. "Baby, your love is priceless."

"You know, Mr. Stratton, sweet words like those will get you anything you want."

He reached over and took her hand in his. "All I want is you, our baby, and that group of furred and finned misfits. How did I get so lucky?"

"My mom poked holes in a package of condoms."

Gray smiled and laid his hand on her stomach. "God, I love that woman."

Next up is One Hundred Whispers

OTHER BOOKS BY KELLY COLLINS

Recipes for Love

A Tablespoon of Temptation

A Pinch of Passion

A Dash of Desire

A Cup of Compassion

A Dollop of Delight

A Layer of Love

Recipe for Love Collection 1-3

The Second Chance Series

Set Free

Set Aside

Set in Stone

Set Up

Set on You

The Second Chance Series Box Set

A Pure Decadence Series

Yours to Have

Yours to Conquer

Yours to Protect

A Pure Decadence Collection

Wilde Love Series

Betting On Him

Betting On Her

Betting On Us

A Wilde Love Collection

The Boys of Fury Series

Redeeming Ryker

Saving Silas

Delivering Decker

The Boys of Fury Boxset

Making the Grade Series

The Dean's List

Honor Roll

The Learning Curve

Making the Grade Box Set

Stand Alone Billionaire Novels

Dream Maker

GET A FREE BOOK.

Go to www.authorkellycollins.com

ABOUT THE AUTHOR

International bestselling author of more than thirty novels, Kelly Collins writes with the intention of keeping love alive. Always a romantic, she blends real-life events with her vivid imagination to create characters and stories that lovers of contemporary romance, new adult, and romantic suspense will return to again and again.

Kelly lives in Colorado at the base of the Rocky Mountains with her husband of twenty-seven years, their two dogs, and a bird that hates her. She has three amazing children, whom she loves to pieces.

For More Information
www.authorkellycollins.com
kelly@authorkellycollins.com

Made in the USA
Monee, IL
06 August 2023

40495913R10164